THE ALIGNMENT ECHO

Navigating First Contact

Mark Anderson, PhD

Selection, Intention, and Restraint

Copyright

First Edition
Printed in the United States of America

ISBN: 978-0-9997340-7-0 (electronic)

ISBN: 978-0-9997340-8-7 (print)

Disclaimer

This novel incorporates real scientific concepts, historical references, astronomical phenomena, and space exploration milestones for narrative purposes. While grounded in established research where possible, all interpretations, extrapolations, technologies, and scenarios presented are speculative and fictional.

Nothing in this work should be construed as technical instruction, scientific guidance, or predictive claim.

Dedication

For those who believe
that patience is a form of intelligence,
and that restraint can carry meaning farther
than speed ever could.

Acknowledgements

This book exists because of curiosity... shared, challenged, and refined.

Thanks to the scientists, linguists, engineers, historians, and explorers whose real work made this story possible. Thanks also to readers who value quiet tension, thoughtful discovery, and stories that trust intelligence more than spectacle.

With gratitude to the engineers and dreamers who launched Voyager 1 (September 5, 1977) and Voyager 2 (August 20, 1977), in pursuit of space exploration.

And to those who understand that some doors open only when we stop trying to force them.

Contents

Preface

This is not a story about first contact.

It is a story about readiness.

Humanity has spent centuries asking whether we are alone in the universe. Far less time has been spent asking whether we would recognize an answer if it arrived quietly... or whether we would mistake patience for absence.

The Alignment Echo explores a different possibility: that intelligence is not measured by how quickly we respond, how far we travel, or how much we claim... but by how carefully we decide when not to act.

The events in this book unfold slowly by design. They reward attention rather than urgency. They suggest that meaning, once rushed, cannot be repaired.

This is a story about listening.

PROLOGUE

The sea was calm, but the stars were not.

They never are, once you learn how to look.

The helmsman loosened his grip on the steering oar and let the ship settle into its course. The wind was steady from the west, warm for the season, carrying the smell of salt and pitch and something faintly metallic from the hull fittings. No clouds. No moon. A perfect night for travel... if one trusted the sky.

He did not trust it blindly.

No one who survived long at sea ever did.

Above him, the stars looked fixed to the untrained eye, nailed into the dark like decorations. But he had learned better. He had learned to see the slow drift, the subtle misalignments, the way certain points returned not to where they had been, but to where they were *meant* to be. Patterns, not positions. Relationships, not points.

That was how you crossed water without landmarks.
That was how you survived absence.

Behind him, the others worked quietly. No songs tonight. No stories. This was not a journey for comfort. In the center of the deck, wrapped in oilcloth and lashed with rope, lay the object they had carried farther than any cargo before it. It was heavy, but not in the way stone should have been. It resisted being moved, as if mass were not the correct word for what it possessed.

It did not glow.
It did not hum.
It did not speak.

That would come later... or not at all.

He knelt beside it and loosened the bindings. The oilcloth fell away to reveal a surface cut unnaturally smooth, darker than the deck beneath it, marked only by shallow incisions... lines, angles, curves that did not form pictures. Not words. Not symbols meant to be read aloud.

They were instructions for *choosing.*

No one aboard fully understood them. That was not required. Understanding came later, if it came at all. What mattered was placement. Orientation. Alignment.

He lifted his gaze back to the sky and checked the stars one last time. Not the bright ones... those were unreliable. He looked instead for what *wasn't* there. Gaps. Voids. The spaces that stayed empty year after year.

Absence was the most stable guide.

When the moment arrived, it felt unremarkable. No sound marked it. No change in the wind. The sea accepted what was given to it without protest, only a deep, muted displacement against the hull. The stars did not shift in response.

The object was released.

It slipped beneath the surface... or perhaps above it. He could not say afterward which direction was correct. Only that it was no longer theirs.

The ship turned east before dawn.

By the time the sun rose, the water where they had stopped was indistinguishable from every other stretch of open sea. No marker. No monument. Nothing to suggest that a decision had been made there that would outlast empires.

He allowed himself one final glance at the sky.

Not to ask whether it had worked.

Only to confirm that the stars were still moving.

They always were.

And somewhere, far beyond the horizon of knowing, something had begun to listen.

CHAPTER 1 — The Tomb That Hummed

The tomb was never supposed to make noise.

Dr. Emilia Kowalska had excavated forty-seven burial sites in her career, and not a single one of them had ever tried to sing to her. For this particular dig, the flatlands stretched out around the trench in long, wind-brushed lines of harvested fields and skeletal trees—the kind of landscape that looked empty until you learned how much history it buried.

She stood at the edge of the trench on the outskirts of **Wyskoć, Poland**, with her helmet clipped to her belt, boots planted in dark mud that had not seen daylight in centuries, listening as the sound returned... low, steady, unmistakable. Not a vibration from machinery. Not wind through stone.

Long before maps, the nearby Warta had been a waterway, meandering but reliable, carrying amber, flint, timber, and the quiet exchange of ideas toward the Baltic.

The faint sound was deeper now. Measured. Almost patient.

"Turn off the generator," she said, without looking back.

"We did," someone replied. A pause. "Twice."

The hum continued.

It wasn't loud. That was the problem. Loud things demanded attention. This didn't. It waited, like it expected to be noticed eventually.

Emilia climbed down into the trench, ignoring the looks from the graduate students hovering at the perimeter. The structure beneath them stretched far longer than any grave had a right to—nearly ten meters of exposed stone, its surface cut flat with a precision that mocked erosion. More specifically, the exposed face measured 9.8 meters in long, 2 meters wide, and averaged forty-seven centimeters thick. No chamber. No offerings. No bones. Just geometry. Clean lines. Sharp alignment.

Emilia had heard strange things before... thermal pops beneath Saharan ruins, wind harmonics in Andean stonework, ice-muffled groans from collapsed chambers in northern Greenland. None of them behaved like this. Those noises wandered. This one returned.

She knelt and placed her palm against the exposed surface.

The sound didn't change.

It didn't react.

It didn't need to.

"This isn't funerary," she said quietly. "Stop calling it a tomb."

"What is it, then?" someone asked.

Emilia didn't answer. She was watching the sunlight creep across the stone, tracing an angle that aligned... too perfectly... with the horizon.

Behind her, a young voice spoke for the first time.

"It's keeping time."

Emilia turned.

The girl stood a little apart from the others, hood up despite the mild weather, eyes fixed not on the structure itself but on the equipment... oscilloscopes, recorders, laptops quietly blinking as if unsure what to make of what they were hearing.

"Time with what?" Emilia asked.

The girl hesitated, then shook her head. "I don't know yet. But it's not random."

The hum dipped... just for an instant... then resumed.

They moved the equipment closer.

This was when Emilia expected the illusion to collapse... some overlooked harmonic, a buried cable, a resonance artifact amplified by expectation. Archaeology taught humility. The earth was clever at lying.

But the readings refused to cooperate.

The microphones recorded a dominant frequency just below the threshold of hearing, steady within a tolerance tighter than most laboratory oscillators. No drift. No decay. No interference from wind, footsteps, or nearby vehicles. When someone dropped a tool into the trench, the spike appeared exactly where it should... *and nowhere else.*

The hum persisted beneath it all.

"It's not acoustic," said Marek, their geophysicist, rubbing at the stubble on his chin. "Or at least not in the way we define sound."

"Seismic?" someone offered.

Marek shook his head. "Wrong profile. Too clean."

Emilia watched Zoë move quietly between the cases, adjusting gain levels, tagging time stamps, running fast Fourier transforms with a speed that suggested habit rather than talent. The girl didn't ask permission. She didn't explain what she was doing.

Zoë adjusted the filters with the calm efficiency of someone who had solved puzzles in hotel rooms on four continents and never once needed to know where she was to understand what she was seeing.

She listened.

"How old did you say the structure was?" Zoë asked, without looking up.

"We don't know yet," Emilia said. "Minimum three thousand years. Possibly older."

Zoë nodded, as if that answered something.

The hum repeated.

Same duration.

Thirty-seven seconds.

Then silence.

Everyone froze.

They waited.

Nothing.

A graduate student exhaled nervously. "Okay. That was... "

The hum returned.

Same strength. Same duration. Same smooth onset and termination, like a switch thrown by something that understood patience.

Zoë's fingers stopped moving.

"It reset," she said.

"What reset?" Emilia asked.

"The interval," Zoë replied. "It's… segmented."

She turned the laptop so Emilia could see. The screen showed a sequence of blocks... time windows stacked neatly, each subdivided into smaller pulses. Not evenly spaced, but not chaotic either. There was internal structure. Hierarchy.

"Like a clock?" Marek asked.

Zoë shook her head. "Clocks drift. This doesn't."

"Then what is it?"

Zoë searched for the word and didn't find one she liked. "It's closer to a pattern that expects continuity."

"That's not an answer," someone muttered.

Zoë glanced up. "Neither is calling it a tomb."

Emilia almost smiled.

By nightfall, the site had changed character.

Floodlights cast harsh shadows across the trench, exaggerating angles that looked intentional now that no one could pretend otherwise. The hum continued, indifferent to the attention it had attracted.

Phones rang. Messages were sent. Permissions were requested retroactively.

Emilia found herself explaining the same thing over and over:

No, it wasn't a burial mound.
No, there were no human remains.
Yes, the alignment appeared intentional.
No, they had not activated anything.

At least, not intentionally.

Zoë sat cross-legged on a folding chair near the equipment, headphones around her neck, eyes unfocused as if listening inward now. She had stopped running analyses. The data was repeating. Perfectly.

"It's not trying to say anything," Zoë said suddenly.

Emilia looked at her. "You're sure?"

"Yes," Zoë said. "Because if it were, there'd be variation. Redundancy. Error correction. This has none of that."

"Then what is it doing?"

Zoë shrugged, a small, almost apologetic motion. "Existing."

The word landed harder than expected.

At 03:33 local time, the hum stopped.

Not gradually. Not as if winding down.

It ended.

Every instrument recorded the same clean cutoff.

Silence settled over the trench, heavy and uncomfortable.

For a long moment, no one spoke.

Then Zoë's laptop chimed softly.

She leaned forward, eyes widening. "That's... new."

Emilia crossed the trench in three strides. "What is?"

Zoë pointed to the time stamp. "It didn't just stop. It completed a cycle."

"A cycle of what?"

Zoë swallowed. "Of itself."

Emilia straightened slowly.

Above them, unseen by anyone on the ground, a satellite passed overhead... its sensors calibrated for weather and terrain, not for patterns that did not announce themselves. Its automated systems logged nothing out of the ordinary.

And far beyond the orbit of that satellite, far beyond the Moon, something that had been placed rather than built registered a change so subtle it would have gone unnoticed by anything less patient than time itself.

The listening state advanced.

CHAPTER 2 — *Thirty-Seven Seconds*

The next night, the hum returned at 03:33.

No one had expected it to.

They had prepared for drift, decay, variation... any of the small mercies that allow a mystery to collapse into something manageable. Instead, the sound arrived exactly when it had ended the night before, with the same gentle onset and the same maddening calm.

Thirty-seven seconds.

Then silence.

Emilia checked her watch without meaning to. She wasn't alone. Half the team had done the same thing, as if time itself had just been caught misbehaving and might bolt if they didn't keep an eye on it.

"That's not coincidence," Marek said finally.

"No," Emilia agreed. "That's scheduling."

The word hung there, uncomfortable.

Zoë didn't speak. She was already pulling up last night's data, overlaying it with the new trace. The two waveforms aligned so perfectly they might as well have been the same recording played twice.

Except they weren't.

"These aren't echoes," Zoë said quietly. "They're iterations."

Someone laughed... too sharp, too quick. "Iterations of what?"

Zoë didn't answer right away. She zoomed in, isolating the internal pulse structure, highlighting a subdivision that hadn't been obvious at first glance. Within the thirty-seven seconds were smaller intervals... uneven, nested, purposeful.

"Of itself," she said at last. "It's repeating because that's what it does."

"That's not how physical systems work," Marek said.

Zoë looked up. "It is if repetition is the point."

By sunrise, the site was awake in a way Emilia had never seen before.

Equipment cases lined the edge of the trench like improvised fortifications. A portable antenna mast had been erected overnight, its presence justified hastily and logged retroactively. Phones buzzed constantly... missed calls, unread messages, requests framed as suggestions that no one pretended could be ignored.

The hum did not return during daylight.

It never had.

That, too, was wrong.

"Environmental trigger?" someone suggested.

"Too clean," Zoë said.

"Human activity suppression?" another offered.

Zoë shook her head. "It's not avoiding us. It's ignoring us."

She brought up a world map on her screen, more out of habit than intention, and let the satellite overlays load. Emilia watched her expression change... not alarm, exactly, but a tightening, as if a hypothesis had just grown teeth.

"Emilia," Zoë said slowly. "Can I borrow your phone?"

Emilia handed it over.

Zoë dialed a number from memory. It rang twice.

"Dr. Al-Hassan," Zoë said when the call connected. "This is Zoë Lin. I need you to check something for me. Right now."

A pause. Then, faintly, a voice edged with amusement. "Zoë, it's nine in the morning."

"Yes," Zoë said. "It is."

She ended the call and turned back to her laptop, fingers moving fast now.

"Who was that?" Emilia asked.

"An astronomer in Oman," Zoë replied. "He owes me a favor."

The confirmation came twelve minutes later.

Dr. Al-Hassan didn't ask why.

He didn't joke.

He simply said, "It's here too."

"What is?" Emilia asked.

There was a brief crackle of interference, then: "A low-frequency signal. Not acoustic. Not electromagnetic in the usual sense. Thirty-seven seconds long."

Emilia closed her eyes.

"Same time?" Zoë asked.

"Yes," Al-Hassan said. "And Zoë... this isn't the first time. It's the first time we noticed."

They stopped pretending it was local after that.

Calls went out quietly... to Chile, to Namibia, to remote observatories that specialized in data no one else wanted. The answers came back unevenly, but the pattern held.

Thirty-seven seconds.
Once per night.
Same window.
Same silence afterward.

Different instruments.
Different continents.

Same behavior.

"This is global," Marek said, staring at the compiled map. "Or... orbital."

Zoë tilted her head. "Or neither."

Emilia studied the trench again, the long stone form cutting through Polish soil with arrogant patience. "Then why here?"

Zoë hesitated. "Because this is where we noticed."

"That's not an answer."

Zoë met her gaze. "It's the only honest one I have."

That night, the hum arrived on schedule.

Everyone stood ready this time... recording, monitoring, measuring in every way they knew how. The signal did not care. It ran its course without deviation, without acknowledgment.

Thirty-seven seconds.

Then silence.

Zoë removed her headphones slowly.

"It's not broadcasting," she said.

Marek frowned. "Then what is it doing?"

Zoë looked at the data one last time, then closed the laptop.

"It's marking something," she said. "Not time. Not location."

"Then what?"

Zoë swallowed. "Progress."

Above the excavation site, far beyond the reach of floodlights or satellites tuned for weather and terrain, something old adjusted a state variable so small it would not register as change to anything that wasn't watching for it.

The count advanced.

CHAPTER 3 — The First Call

The first official call arrived at 09:07.

It didn't come through the site coordinator. It didn't come through the regional heritage office, or the university, or any of the channels Emilia understood well enough to mistrust properly.

It came through Marek's phone.

He glanced at the caller ID, frowned, and held it out to Emilia as if the device had begun misbehaving on its own.

"Warsaw," he said. "But not… the usual Warsaw."

Emilia took the phone. The number was long, sterile, and unfamiliar… one of those lines that belonged to buildings with no signage and people who never gave their full names.

She answered anyway.

"Dr. Kowalska," a voice said at once, crisp and unnervingly calm. "This is Deputy Director Rudzki, National Security Bureau. You are leading the excavation at Wyskoć."

It wasn't a question.

"Yes," Emilia said carefully. "This is an archaeological site."

There was a pause… small, deliberate, like punctuation.

"We understand you have discovered an anomaly."

Emilia could almost hear a file being opened.

"How would you like me to define anomaly?" she asked.

The voice didn't shift. "We will define it for you. You will confirm or deny. Is your team recording a recurring low-frequency signal with a fixed duration?"

Emilia looked across the trench. Zoë sat on an overturned equipment case, knees pulled to her chest, watching the field beyond the floodlights as if the horizon might answer questions the data couldn't.

Emilia spoke slowly. "We are measuring a repeatable signal. Yes."

"And is this signal present only at your site?"

Emilia didn't answer immediately.

She heard Zoë's voice in her head: *Because this is where we noticed.*

"No," Emilia said. "It appears to be broader."

Another pause. Slightly longer.

"You have shared data externally."

It wasn't phrased as a accusation. It felt like a statement of physics.

Emilia's stomach tightened. "With scientific colleagues. For verification."

"Do you have a list of recipients?"

"Not compiled," Emilia said, and forced herself not to add *yet.*

The voice softened by a fraction... not kinder, just smoother.

"Doctor, you are not in trouble. But you are now in a category. In this category, we proceed differently."

Emilia stared at the long stone shape, the trench, the carefully brushed soil, as if she might find the word *category* hidden in the sediment.

"What do you want from us?" she asked.

"Containment," the voice said. "First. Understanding, later. You will suspend all external communications and prepare an inventory of personnel, equipment, and collected data. A team will arrive within twelve hours."

"Within... " Emilia began.

"Doctor," the voice said gently, "this is not a request."

The line went dead.

Marek watched her face. "Bad?"

Emilia handed the phone back. "Official."

He swore under his breath in Polish. "We're done. They'll shut it down."

"They can try," Zoë said from across the trench.

Emilia turned. "What did you say?"

Zoë stood, hands shoved into her hoodie pocket. Her tone was flat, but her eyes weren't. "They can shut down *us*. They can shut down the lights and the generator and the cameras. They can put a tarp over the trench."

She nodded toward the stone.

"But they can't shut down that."

Marek let out a short laugh. "You sound very confident for someone who hasn't explained what it is."

Zoë didn't flinch. "Because it doesn't care what we think it is."

Emilia felt something like relief and something like fear in the same breath.

"Okay," Emilia said. "Then we work fast."

They spent the morning turning the site into something it had never been meant to be: a laboratory that looked like a trench and a trench that acted like an instrument.

The hum itself was cooperative only in the way gravity is cooperative. It repeated at night. It did not repeat when asked. It did not change in response to stimulus. They tried anyway, because scientists and archaeologists were both trained to offend the universe politely until it admitted something.

They placed sensors along the length of the structure, mapping vibration gradients across stone and soil. They measured ambient electromagnetic fields, just to rule out the embarrassing. They monitored temperature shifts and barometric pressure. They ran controlled tests with speakers and transducers to see if they could induce sympathetic harmonics.

Nothing touched it.

The signal did not smear.

It did not wobble.

It did not care.

Zoë drew in a notebook while the others argued. Not pictures. Not diagrams of the trench. Something stranger: nested brackets, intervals marked by dots, small lines grouped into sets of uneven count.

Emilia leaned over her shoulder. "What is that?"

Zoë's pencil paused. "A way to not forget."

"That's not an answer."

Zoë glanced up. "It's not for you. Not yet."

Emilia straightened, forcing herself to breathe through the irritation. She had dealt with prodigies before... usually older, usually male, usually funded.

Zoë was neither funded nor smug. That made her worse, somehow.

At noon, an email arrived that made Marek go pale.

It wasn't from Warsaw.

It was from the European Space Agency.

Subject line:

REQUEST FOR COORDINATION — ANOMALOUS SIGNAL EVENT

Emilia read it twice.

"How did they... " Marek began.

Zoë looked over her shoulder. "Because we weren't the only ones who noticed."

Emilia's mouth went dry. "ESA noticed?"

Zoë shrugged. "Or someone who watches ESA's telemetry. Or someone who watches the people who watch ESA's telemetry."

Marek stared at her. "How do you talk like that?"

Zoë's expression didn't change. "Practice."

Emilia forced herself back into motion. "What does it say?"

Marek scrolled. "They want data. They want our time stamps. They want instrument profiles. And they want… us not to share it publicly until they 'characterize the event.'"

Emilia let out a short, humorless sound. "So everyone is coordinating silently."

"Yes," Marek said.

"No," Zoë corrected gently. "Everyone is panicking politely."

The first of the new vehicles arrived at 15:22.

Black. Matte. Unmarked. Too clean for rural Poland.

A second followed. Then a third.

The convoy rolled to a stop beneath the ash trees and sat there for a moment as if waiting for permission from the landscape itself.

Emilia climbed out of the trench and wiped her hands on her trousers, ignoring the mud. She felt an old familiar anger… the kind that came when bureaucracy tried to step on discovery because discovery didn't fill out the right forms.

A man stepped out of the lead vehicle.

He wasn't wearing a uniform. That would have been easier. He wore a dark coat that looked expensive and forgettable at the same time, like it had been designed to be overlooked.

He removed his sunglasses.

His eyes were pale.

He looked at the trench, then at Emilia, then... too briefly... at Zoë.

"Dr. Kowalska," he said.

Emilia didn't offer her hand. "And you are?"

"Dr. Elias Thorne," he replied. The accent was not Polish. The name was not Polish either, and the way he said it suggested he didn't care if she noticed.

He smiled, faintly. "I'm here to help you keep your discovery."

"That's not what your people said on the phone," Emilia said.

"My people," Thorne repeated, as if tasting the phrase. "Yes. They do tend to lead with containment."

He looked past her, into the trench. The hum wasn't active now, but Thorne's attention moved as if it were.

"You've been calling it a tomb," he said.

Emilia's jaw tightened. "We stopped."

"Good," Thorne said. "Because it isn't."

He stepped closer to the trench edge and crouched, studying the exposed stone face with the focus of someone who understood geometry not as art but as language.

Zoë walked up beside Emilia without being invited.

"You're late," Zoë said.

Thorne didn't look surprised. "Am I?"

"You already knew," Zoë pressed.

Thorne finally turned to her. His gaze was steady, neither dismissive nor impressed... just assessing, like an instrument reading.

"I suspected," he said.

Zoë held his eyes. "Of what?"

Thorne's smile returned, thinner this time. "That something would start counting again."

Emilia felt a cold line of tension slide down her spine.

"Counting what?" she asked.

Thorne looked at the trench.

Then at the sky.

Then back at Emilia, as if deciding how much truth a human could carry without dropping it.

"I don't know," he said, and for the first time his voice wasn't smooth. It was careful. "But I know this... whatever it is, it isn't waking up."

He paused.

"It's checking whether we have."

CHAPTER 4 — Angles That Shouldn't Agree

The stone did not behave like stone.

That was the first thing Emilia realized once the initial chaos of authority and containment settled into something resembling routine. Archaeological sites had habits. Materials had tolerances. Time left fingerprints that, once learned, repeated everywhere.

This structure refused to cooperate.

They began with the basics.

Laser levels traced the length of the exposed surface, projecting thin red lines across stone faces smoothed with a precision no local culture should have possessed. The measurements came back wrong in ways that were consistent enough to be irritating.

"Recheck the baseline," Emilia said.

"We did," Marek replied. "Three times."

"Then do it again."

They did.

Marek Nowak didn't raise his voice when the numbers came back wrong. He never did. Years spent mapping fault lines in Iceland, running seismic arrays beneath the Andes, and chasing ghost signals through decommissioned Soviet tunnels had trained that habit out of him. When Marek said something didn't make sense, it wasn't excitement speaking... it was experience.

He recalibrated the laser levels anyway. Again.

"Stone drifts," he said, mostly to himself. "Ground settles. Everything argues with time."

He glanced up at the readout, then frowned.

"This one isn't arguing."

The angles didn't drift. They didn't wander. They *agreed*... with one another, across distances that should have accumulated error. The long axis of the structure aligned neither perfectly north nor with any known cardinal compromise used in regional construction.

"It's not solar," Marek said. "At least not directly."

Emilia crouched near the eastern edge, watching how the late afternoon light slid across the surface. "Then it's not about where the sun is. It's about where it *isn't*."

Zoë had been quiet since Thorne's arrival. Too quiet. She moved along the trench with the same careful steps she used when solving problems that didn't want to be rushed, stopping every few meters to mark something in her notebook.

"What are you tracking?" Emilia asked.

Zoë hesitated, then showed her the page.

It wasn't a sketch of the trench. It was a grid... not square, not circular, but something between. Lines intersected at uneven intervals, forming clusters rather than rows. Some intersections were marked. Others were deliberately left blank.

"This isn't geometry," Emilia said.

Zoë shook her head. "It's relationships."

"That's worse."

Zoë almost smiled.

By late afternoon, Thorne joined them in the trench.

He didn't announce himself. He didn't need to. Conversations thinned the way they did when someone accustomed to being obeyed entered a room without asking permission first.

Emilia noted the details automatically. No university badge. No visible credentials. Shoes too clean for the site, but worn in a way that suggested long travel rather than caution. The kind of man who never introduced himself twice, because people tended to remember the first time.

Marek stiffened when he saw him.

That reaction mattered more than anything Thorne said.

"Dr. Elias Thorne," he offered, eventually, as if remembering manners from another context. "I consult on anomalous signal events."

Emilia arched an eyebrow. "That's not a discipline."

Thorne smiled faintly. "It is if you've seen enough of them."

He crouched near the exposed stone, careful not to touch it, eyes moving with the practiced economy of someone who understood geometry as consequence rather than design.

"You're measuring it like a structure," he said.

Emilia crossed her arms. "That's what it is."

Thorne didn't look at her. "It's also a filter."

Zoë glanced up sharply.

Emilia felt it then... the reason Warsaw had escalated so quickly. Thorne wasn't here to observe.

He was here because something, somewhere, had decided this no longer belonged to archaeology alone.

He moved carefully, avoiding equipment, stepping only where others had already stepped. He still hadn't touched the stone, and Emilia couldn't decide whether that restraint was respectful or calculated.

"You've found alignments," he said.

"Yes," Emilia replied. "That shouldn't exist."

"That always depends on your reference frame," Thorne said.

Marek snorted. "We tried north. We tried solar. We tried stellar."

"And Earth?" Thorne asked.

Emilia looked up sharply. "What do you mean?"

28

Thorne gestured vaguely at the sky. "All of those assume Earth is the center of relevance."

Zoë's pencil froze.

Emilia felt a slow tightening in her chest. "Everything we build assumes Earth."

"Yes," Thorne said. "Which is why this stands out."

Zoë stood abruptly and moved to her tablet, pulling up the site scans. She overlaid the incisions, then rotated the composite... not to match Earth's orientation, but to remove it entirely.

The shapes shifted.

They didn't resolve into a map.

They resolved into **relationships**.

"Oh," Zoë breathed.

Marek leaned in. "What?"

"These shapes aren't pointing *to* anything," Zoë said. "They're pointing *between* things."

"That's nonsense."

"No," Zoë said quietly. "It's navigation without destinations."

––

By dusk, they had uncovered more of the surface... enough to reveal shallow incisions that had been invisible under sediment. They were subtle, worn nearly smooth by time, but unmistakably intentional.

Lines.
Angles.
Curves that didn't quite close.

"They're not decorative," Marek said.

"They're not writing either," Emilia replied.

Thorne stood at the edge of the trench, hands clasped behind his back, observing without interfering. He hadn't touched anything. He hadn't asked permission. That bothered Emilia more than if he had done both.

"These markings don't repeat," Emilia continued. "No motif. No symmetry."

Zoë leaned closer, eyes scanning the stone. "They do repeat," she said. "Just not locally."

She pointed to one curve near the center. Then another, farther down the trench. Then another, near the western edge.

"They're the same," she said. "But only if you ignore scale."

Marek frowned. "Ignore scale?"

Zoë nodded. "Same shape. Different size. Different orientation. Like… references."

"To what?" Emilia asked.

Zoë didn't answer. She stepped back and pulled up the site scans on her tablet, overlaying the incisions digitally. When she adjusted transparency, the shapes aligned… not perfectly, but meaningfully.

They didn't stack.

They *nested*.

Emilia felt a familiar chill… the kind that came when something clicked but refused to explain itself.

"This isn't a map," Emilia said slowly.

Zoë shook her head. "It's instructions for making one."

Night fell cleanly, as it often did in rural Poland. The lights came on. The trench glowed stark and artificial against the surrounding dark.

The hum did not return yet.

Zoë sat cross-legged near the eastern edge, tablet balanced on her knees, rotating the composite overlay in slow increments. Emilia watched her for a long moment before speaking.

"Say it," Emilia said.

Zoë didn't look up. "Say what?"

"What you're thinking but haven't said because it sounds insane."

Zoë exhaled. "It's not oriented to Earth."

Silence followed... thick, deliberate.

Marek broke it first. "Everything is oriented to Earth. That's what orientation means."

Zoë finally looked up. "No. Everything we *build* is oriented to Earth. This isn't built for us."

Thorne shifted slightly. Just enough for Emilia to notice.

Zoë continued. "If you treat Earth as the reference point, the alignments don't resolve. But if you treat Earth as *one point among many*..."

She rotated the overlay again. The nested shapes began to suggest something else entirely... not positions, but *transitions*. Movements between regions. Absences treated as anchors.

"This isn't saying 'look here,'" Zoë said. "It's saying 'move like this.'"

Emilia felt her pulse quicken. "Like navigation."

Zoë nodded. "But not on land. And not at sea."

They all looked up.

The stars were sharp tonight, cold and exact.

Thorne spoke at last.

"Maps that show destinations go obsolete," he said quietly. "Maps that show *how to choose* endure."

Emilia turned on him. "You knew."

Thorne met her gaze. "I suspected."

31

"From what?"

Thorne hesitated... just a fraction. "From things that didn't resolve when they should have."

Zoë closed her tablet.

"The hum isn't the message," she said. "It's the metronome."

Emilia swallowed. "For what?"

Zoë looked back at the stone, at the angles that shouldn't agree, at the structure that had waited longer than any monument had a right to.

"For steps," she said.

At 03:33, the hum returned.

Thirty-seven seconds.

But this time, one of the sensors registered something new... not louder, not stronger.

Aligned.

A correlation between the signal phase and the incisions in the stone.

Zoë's tablet chimed softly.

She stared at the screen, then up at the stars, then back down again.

"It's updating," she whispered.

Emilia felt the weight of centuries press in around them.

"Updating what?"

Zoë didn't answer.

She didn't need to.

CHAPTER 5 — *This Didn't Start Here*

The email arrived without urgency.

That was what made it dangerous.

It didn't carry the usual flags... no red banners, no priority tags, no language that demanded immediate action. It slid into Emilia's inbox at 06:18 local time, timestamped from Paris, addressed personally, and written as if everyone involved had already agreed on the nature of the problem.

REQUEST FOR COORDINATION... HISTORICAL SIGNAL ANOMALY

Emilia read it once, then again, then forwarded it to Marek and Zoë without comment.

Outside, the site was quiet. Too quiet. The hum had ended hours earlier, leaving behind a silence that felt provisional, like a pause rather than a conclusion. Morning fog clung to the low fields beyond the fencing, softening the horizon until Poland looked smaller than it had any right to.

Thorne was already awake.

He stood near the eastern edge of the trench, hands in his coat pockets, watching the fog thin as the sun rose. He didn't turn when Emilia approached.

"You've heard," he said.

"I've read," Emilia replied. "You knew this was coming."

Thorne smiled faintly. "I hoped it wouldn't be today."

They gathered in the temporary operations tent just after seven.

Marek brought the overnight data. Zoë brought her notebook. Thorne brought nothing at all.

The call connected on the second ring.

A woman appeared on the screen... early forties, composed, the kind of posture that came from years of speaking to rooms that expected clarity more than warmth.

"Dr. Kowalska," she said. "I'm Claire Montagne, European Space Agency. Thank you for agreeing to coordinate."

Claire Montagne didn't introduce herself beyond her name, but the way the call had been routed... direct, unfiltered, bypassing three normal layers of review... told Emilia everything she needed to know.

"We didn't agree," Emilia said evenly. "We were informed."

Montagne inclined her head. "Yes. I'm aware of the distinction."

She tapped something offscreen. The image shifted, replaced by a graph... clean, spare, unmistakably real.

"This is what we noticed," Montagne continued. "Or rather, what we finally recognized."

The graph showed a low-frequency trace.

Thirty-seven seconds long.

Marek leaned forward. "That's ours."

"Yes," Montagne said. "And no."

The graph duplicated itself. Then again. Three traces, perfectly aligned.

"Different instruments," Montagne said. "Different missions. Different decades."

Zoë's breath caught. "Decades?"

Montagne nodded. "We went back. Farther than we should have, frankly. Into archival telemetry that no one has reviewed by hand since it was recorded."

She paused.

"One of the signals predates your excavation by forty-eight years."

Silence swallowed the tent.

Marek was the first to speak. "That's impossible."

"It was unnoticed," Montagne corrected. "Because no one was looking for repetition."

Emilia felt the slow, sinking realization take shape. "Which mission."

Montagne hesitated. Just long enough.

"Voyager," she said.

The name landed heavily.

Not because it was dramatic... but because it was familiar. Domestic. Voyager was a relic of optimism, a message in a bottle launched when humanity still believed the universe would be impressed by gold-plated greetings and curated playlists.

Zoë stared at the screen. "Which one?"

"Both," Montagne replied. "But Voyager 2 recorded it first."

She switched displays.

A grainy plot filled the screen, its resolution crude by modern standards, its margins annotated in the neat handwriting of engineers who never imagined anyone would look again.

"There," Montagne said, highlighting a segment. "1977. Outside the heliosphere. A low-frequency fluctuation flagged and discarded as background noise."

The trace lasted thirty-seven seconds.

Zoë's fingers tightened around her notebook.

"They didn't know what it was," Montagne continued. "Neither did we. Not until now."

Thorne spoke softly from the back of the tent. "Because you didn't know what to compare it to."

Montagne glanced at him. "Exactly."

She pulled up another trace. Then another.

"Different years. Different distances. Same structure. Same internal segmentation."

Marek swallowed. "It's not coming from the spacecraft."

"No," Montagne said. "It never was."

"Then what... " Emilia began.

Montagne held up a hand. "We don't know. But we know this much."

She leaned closer to the camera.

"It didn't originate near Earth."

The call ended without ceremony.

No instructions. No demands. Just a quiet agreement to keep talking.

For a long moment, no one in the tent moved.

Zoë broke the silence.

"We're not early," she said.

Marek looked at her. "What?"

"We're late," Zoë replied. "This has been running longer than we've been alive. Longer than anyone here."

Emilia felt a tightness in her chest. "Then why now?"

Zoë opened her notebook and flipped to a page filled with the nested structures she'd been drawing since the first night.

"Because something changed," she said. "Not the signal."

She tapped the page.

"Us."

Thorne stepped forward at last.

"This is the part people get wrong," he said. "They hear 'first contact' and imagine voices, lights, answers."

He looked at the stone through the tent opening, at the structure that had waited quietly beneath Polish soil while empires rose and fell above it.

"This isn't contact," he continued. "It's verification."

Marek frowned. "Verification of what?"

Thorne met his eyes. "That we can recognize something that doesn't announce itself."

Zoë closed her notebook slowly. "That we can follow steps without being told where they lead."

Thorne nodded. "Exactly."

Outside, the fog had lifted completely.

The site looked ordinary again... mud, fencing, equipment, the long stone shape resting inert and patient in the ground.

Emilia knew better now.

"Voyager wasn't a message," she said quietly.

"No," Thorne agreed. "It was a listener."

Zoë's voice was barely above a whisper. "And so is this."

Somewhere beyond the reach of Earth's instruments, beyond the path of its bravest machines, a process older than memory registered another completed interval.

The count did not accelerate.

It did not slow.

It simply continued.

CHAPTER 6 — The First Step

The mistake was small.

That was the problem.

Zoë didn't notice it at first because it looked exactly like the kind of thing she did dozens of times a day... adjusting a parameter not to provoke a response, but to clarify a pattern. She wasn't trying to communicate. She wasn't trying to test the structure.

She was trying to remove noise.

The hum had ended hours earlier, leaving behind its usual residue of silence and anticipation. The site was awake but subdued, as if everyone were waiting for something they didn't want to admit they expected.

Zoë sat alone at the equipment table, notebook open beside her laptop, the nested interval diagrams growing denser with each iteration. She had begun labeling them... not with numbers, but with relationships. If this interval shortened, that one widened. If this cluster tightened, another loosened elsewhere.

It wasn't language.

It was balance.

She frowned and adjusted the timing gate on one of the filters, narrowing the window by a fraction... less than a millisecond. The change was insignificant by any normal standard. It wouldn't alter the signal. It couldn't.

The screen flickered.

Zoë froze.

The data stream recompiled itself... not dramatically, not with alarms or spikes, but with a subtle reordering of the internal pulses. The thirty-seven-second envelope remained intact.

Inside it, something shifted.

Her heart began to race.

"That's… new," she whispered.

The hum did not return.

Instead, something else happened.

One of the alignment sensors... positioned along the eastern edge of the structure... registered a phase correlation that had not appeared before. Not stronger. Not weaker.

Earlier.

Zoë stood so abruptly her chair toppled backward.

"Emilia," she called, forcing her voice to stay even. "Can you come here?"

Emilia arrived quickly, Marek close behind. Thorne watched from a distance, expression unreadable.

Zoë turned the laptop toward them. "I didn't trigger it," she said immediately. "I wasn't trying to."

Marek squinted at the display. "Trigger what?"

Zoë swallowed. "I changed a filter. That's all. I was cleaning up the data."

"And?" Emilia asked.

"And the internal segmentation… rebalanced."

Marek stared. "That's impossible. Filters don't affect sources."

Zoë nodded. "I know."

Thorne stepped closer.

"Show me," he said.

Zoë replayed the sequence. The before-and-after traces overlaid cleanly... too cleanly. The difference wasn't amplitude or frequency.

It was *timing*.

Thorne exhaled slowly. "You stepped into it."

Zoë looked up sharply. "What?"

"You didn't send a signal," Thorne said. "You aligned yourself with one."

They argued for nearly an hour.

Not loudly. Not emotionally. This was the kind of argument that happened when everyone involved knew the stakes were already higher than comfort allowed.

"It could be coincidence," Marek insisted.

"Coincidence doesn't rebalance nested structures," Zoë replied.

"We don't know that," Emilia said.

Zoë met her gaze. "We do now."

Thorne watched them with an expression Zoë couldn't quite place... something between concern and confirmation.

"This is what happened with Voyager," he said at last.

The tent went still.

"Voyager didn't transmit anything new," Thorne continued. "It didn't send a message. It didn't provoke a response."

He gestured toward Zoë's screen.

"It *listened* in the right way."

That night, Zoë dreamed of a room she had never seen.

It wasn't large. It wasn't small. It had no walls in the usual sense... just boundaries defined by absence. Shapes hovered in it, not solid, not luminous, arranged in relationships rather than positions.

She moved through the room without walking.

Each time she adjusted her path, the room adjusted with her.

She woke before dawn with the uneasy certainty that the dream hadn't been imagination so much as *practice*.

The Voyager data arrived just after breakfast.

Not through ESA. Not through Warsaw.

Through Thorne.

He didn't explain how he had it. He simply placed a drive on the table and waited.

Emilia loaded it on an isolated system.

The telemetry was crude, as Montagne had warned... low resolution, sparse, annotated by engineers who had no idea what they were looking at. But once Zoë overlaid the archival data with their own, the similarity was undeniable.

Same envelope.
Same segmentation.
Same internal logic.

But there was one difference.

Voyager's signal lacked the rebalancing Zoë had just observed.

"It never crossed the threshold," Zoë said quietly.

Marek frowned. "Threshold of what?"

Zoë hesitated. "Participation."

Thorne nodded once. "Voyager could listen. It couldn't *adjust.*"

Zoë's hands trembled slightly. She folded them together to hide it.

"You're saying I did something Voyager couldn't."

"Yes," Thorne said. "Accidentally."

Emilia felt a chill. "Then what happens if she does it on purpose?"

No one answered.

41

That night, at 03:33, the hum returned.

Thirty-seven seconds.

But this time, Zoë didn't watch the clock.

She watched the structure.

As the hum progressed, the alignment markers she'd mapped earlier began to correlate... not physically, not visibly, but mathematically. The nested relationships tightened, resolving into something that felt less like a pattern and more like a *path*.

Zoë adjusted nothing.

She didn't need to.

The hum ended.

The sensors chirped softly.

Zoë stared at the screen, pulse roaring in her ears.

"It's waiting," she said.

"For what?" Emilia asked.

Zoë swallowed. "For the next step."

Thorne's voice was low, almost reverent.

"Then don't rush it," he said. "Whatever built this didn't."

Zoë leaned back in her chair, staring at the ceiling of the tent, suddenly aware of the weight pressing gently but unmistakably against her chest.

She had crossed something.

Not a boundary.

A role.

She wasn't just observing anymore.

She was being *counted*.

CHAPTER 7 — The Weight of Waiting

The first argument didn't sound like an argument.

It sounded like logistics.

They stood in the operations tent with coffee cooling in their hands and mud drying on their boots, discussing power budgets, sensor drift, and how long the generators could run before someone higher up asked uncomfortable questions about fuel receipts.

No one mentioned the word *step*.

But everyone was thinking it.

Zoë sat at the table, notebook closed now, hands wrapped around a paper cup she hadn't touched. She had learned something new about herself in the last twenty-four hours, and it wasn't flattering.

She wanted to try again.

That scared her more than the hum ever had.

Marek broke first.

"We shouldn't repeat it," he said, not looking at Zoë. "Accidental is one thing. Intentional is something else."

Zoë kept her voice steady. "You repeat experiments all the time."

"Yes," Marek said. "When we understand the system."

Thorne leaned against the tent pole, arms folded. He hadn't spoken yet. That, too, was information.

Emilia watched them both, the familiar weight of responsibility settling into her shoulders. This was the moment archaeology textbooks never covered... the one where discovery stopped being about the past and started being about consequences.

"What happens if we don't?" she asked.

No one answered immediately.

Outside, the site was quiet. Too quiet. The stone lay inert, unimpressed by human hesitation.

Zoë stared at the table. "It will still happen," she said finally. "Just without us paying attention."

Marek shook his head. "That's an assumption."

Zoë looked up. "So is safety."

The call came just after noon.

This time it wasn't Warsaw or ESA.

It was a video feed routed through Thorne's equipment, the kind that didn't leave logs unless someone wanted them to.

Three faces appeared.

None of them introduced themselves.

They didn't need to.

Emilia recognized the posture immediately... people accustomed to making decisions that never became headlines.

"You have something you don't understand," one of them said.

Emilia folded her arms. "That's called research."

The woman on the screen didn't smile. "That's called exposure."

Marek leaned forward. "You've seen the data."

"Yes," the woman replied. "Enough to know that you're standing too close to it."

Zoë felt something tighten in her chest.

Thorne finally spoke. "They didn't cause it."

"We're not concerned with cause," the woman said. "We're concerned with amplification."

Zoë's cup crumpled slightly in her grip.

Emilia noticed.

"So what," Emilia said, "you shut us down?"

The man beside the woman answered. "We slow you down."

"How?"

"By making sure no one makes decisions alone."

Zoë looked up sharply.

"That includes her," the man added, nodding toward Zoë.

The tent felt suddenly smaller.

After the call ended, no one spoke for a long moment.

Marek rubbed his face. "They're right, you know."

Zoë flinched. "About what?"

"About amplification," Marek said. "Whatever this is, it's sensitive to alignment. If we push... "

"I didn't push," Zoë said.

"No," Marek agreed softly. "You *matched.*"

That word hung there, heavier than any accusation.

Emilia turned to Thorne. "You've been quiet."

Thorne met her gaze. "Because this is the point where people start lying to themselves."

"About what?"

"About who's in control."

Zoë stood abruptly, chair scraping the floor.

"I don't want to be special," she said, voice tight. "I don't want this to be about me."

Thorne nodded. "It isn't."

That didn't help.

That evening, Zoë walked the perimeter of the site alone.

The fencing hummed faintly in the breeze. Beyond it, fields stretched out under a sky that looked too big to care about human fear. The stars were coming out early, sharp and indifferent.

She stopped near the eastern edge, where the alignment had first tightened.

She didn't bring her notebook.

She didn't bring her laptop.

She just stood there.

If this were a test, she thought, *what would it be testing?*

Intelligence? No.
Curiosity? Too easy.
Courage? Too romantic.

Patience.

The realization settled slowly.

The structure didn't react to force.
It didn't reward speed.
It didn't respond to noise.

It responded to *restraint*.

Zoë exhaled.

She wasn't supposed to act.

She was supposed to wait... *correctly*.

At 03:33, the hum returned.

Thirty-seven seconds.

This time, no one rushed for instruments.

They listened.

Not to the sound... but to the space around it. The way it filled the trench without dominating it. The way it ended without drama.

When it stopped, nothing else happened.

No shift.
No update.
No response.

Marek let out a breath he hadn't realized he was holding. "Good."

Zoë nodded slowly. "Yes."

Thorne watched her carefully. "You didn't step."

Zoë shook her head. "I didn't need to."

"And?"

"And it didn't punish us for that."

Emilia frowned. "You were expecting punishment?"

Zoë hesitated. "I don't think it punishes. I think it... notes."

The word sent a quiet chill through the tent.

Thorne spoke softly. "Then tonight mattered."

"How?" Emilia asked.

Thorne looked at the stone.

"Because waiting is also a choice."

Zoë sat down, suddenly exhausted.

She understood now.

The next step wasn't about intelligence.

It was about whether humanity could resist the urge to prove itself.

And somewhere, far beyond Earth's impatience, the count continued... not faster, not slower.

Just steadily.

CHAPTER 8 — The Wrong Way to Listen

The first failure didn't happen in Poland.

It happened in Nevada.

They called it a calibration error at first. That was the polite fiction that let everyone keep working without admitting what had gone wrong. A private research array... well-funded, well-instrumented, and very confident... had attempted to reproduce the Wyskoć alignment using a scaled model and a deliberately aggressive signal-matching routine.

They forced the timing.

They amplified the response.

They waited.

For thirty-seven seconds, nothing happened.

Then the array went dark.

Not catastrophically. Not dramatically. Just... offline. No surge. No heat signature. No physical damage. The systems rebooted cleanly, logs intact but meaningless... timestamps misaligned, internal clocks desynchronized by fractions too small to explain and too large to ignore.

The report arrived in Emilia's inbox at 05:42, stamped **CONFIDENTIAL** and written in the careful language of people who didn't want to be blamed.

Marek read it twice.

"They pushed," he said quietly.

Zoë nodded. "They stepped without listening."

Thorne didn't look surprised.

The second fracture was closer to home.

It surfaced not as an argument, but as a proposal.

49

A thin document circulated through channels that didn't officially exist, outlining a controlled escalation protocol. More power. Tighter alignment. Shortened intervals. A schedule.

Someone had even named it.

ACTIVE ENGAGEMENT PHASE.

Emilia stared at the document in silence.

"They want to provoke it," Marek said.

"They want to *confirm* it," Emilia replied. "Those are not the same thing."

Zoë scanned the proposal without touching it, as if proximity alone might matter. "They think this is a system you interrogate."

Thorne folded his arms. "That's how humans treat silence. As something to be corrected."

"And you?" Emilia asked.

Thorne met her gaze. "I've seen what happens when patience is mistaken for passivity."

That night, Zoë didn't stay in the tent.

She sat at the edge of the trench, boots dangling over centuries-old stone, notebook closed beside her like an offering she wasn't ready to give back. The air was cold, sharp enough to clear the noise from her thoughts.

She wasn't afraid anymore.

That worried her.

At 03:33, the hum returned.

Thirty-seven seconds.

Zoë didn't analyze it.

She watched.

Not the stone. Not the instruments. The *intervals between her own breaths.*

Something felt... different.

Not louder.
Not clearer.
Closer.

When the hum ended, the silence didn't rush in the way it usually did. It lingered, held, like the pause at the end of a question that hadn't been answered yet.

Zoë's tablet chirped softly.

She frowned and glanced down.

One of the alignment models had updated... not structurally, not numerically, but *relationally*. A connection she hadn't drawn was now highlighted, as if the system were gently suggesting a better way to look at what she already had.

Zoë's pulse quickened.

She hadn't changed anything.

She hadn't stepped.

She hadn't *asked*.

The report from Nevada triggered exactly the reaction Emilia had expected and feared.

Meetings multiplied. Access narrowed. Language hardened.

Words like *containment, risk*, and *control* replaced *pattern* and *structure*. The people who had listened first were slowly outnumbered by people who wanted results they could point to.

Marek slammed his tablet down harder than he meant to. "They're going to break it."

Emilia didn't argue.

Thorne spoke instead. "No," he said. "They're going to prove they don't understand it."

Zoë looked up. "Is that… bad?"

Thorne considered the question. "It depends on whether the thing doing the observing values intelligence… or restraint."

Just before dawn, Zoë showed Emilia the updated model.

"It changed," Zoë said.

Emilia frowned. "You updated it?"

Zoë shook her head. "It did."

Marek leaned in. "That's not possible."

Zoë didn't smile. "Neither was the first hum."

The highlighted connection wasn't dramatic. It didn't spell anything out. It simply suggested a path that avoided force entirely… a gentler alignment, slower, less efficient by human standards.

"It's showing us the *wrong* way," Emilia said slowly.

Zoë nodded. "Because that's the way we keep trying."

Thorne looked at the model, then at Zoë.

"It rewarded you," he said.

Zoë swallowed. "For what?"

"For waiting," Thorne replied.

That evening, the Nevada array remained silent.

No further anomalies. No second chance.

The proposal for Active Engagement stalled… not canceled, but slowed, trapped in committee and caution.

And at Wyskoć, beneath Polish soil that had learned patience long before humans had words for it, the structure rested as it always had.

Except now, something had changed.

Not the hum.

Not the stone.

The *relationship*.

Zoë felt it as she packed up her notebook, a quiet certainty settling in her chest.

This wasn't about passing a test.

It was about whether humanity could learn to stop mistaking urgency for intelligence.

Somewhere beyond the reach of forced signals and hurried minds, the count advanced again.

Not because someone had pushed.

But because someone had finally learned how not to.

CHAPTER 9 — Competing Definitions of Caution

The disagreement began with a whiteboard.

It stood at the far end of the operations tent, hastily cleaned of yesterday's equations and diagrams, now bearing three columns written in precise block letters:

OBSERVE
INTERACT
INTERVENE

No one remembered who had written them. That, in itself, was telling.

Emilia stood with her arms folded, scanning the list as if it might rearrange itself under scrutiny. Marek sat at the table, fingers laced, expression unreadable. Thorne leaned against a support pole, eyes moving not between the words but between the people reading them.

Zoë remained seated, notebook closed.

"We are not voting," Emilia said calmly. "This is not a democratic process."

"No," Marek agreed. "It's a methodological one."

A man from Warsaw... introduced only as *Piotr*... cleared his throat. "Methodology presumes shared risk tolerance."

Emilia turned to him. "Then let's define the risks."

They did.

That was the remarkable thing.

Instead of raised voices, there were lists. Instead of accusations, there were assumptions laid bare and examined one by one. Power budgets. Failure modes. Containment scenarios. The Nevada incident was referenced precisely once, not as a warning, but as a data point.

"They forced alignment," Marek said. "We didn't."

"They accelerated the interval," Zoë added. "We didn't."

"They assumed response was the goal," Thorne said. "We didn't."

Piotr nodded, jotting notes. "And yet something changed here."

Zoë looked up. "Yes."

"How?"

"I waited," Zoë said. "Correctly."

No one laughed.

The ESA joined remotely.

Claire Montagne appeared on-screen again, posture unchanged, eyes alert. This time, she was not alone. Two additional windows opened beside hers... one from a deep-space tracking facility in Argentina, another from a satellite operations center whose location was not identified.

Montagne listened as Emilia summarized their findings.

When Emilia finished, Montagne said, "Your position is that restraint constitutes engagement."

"Yes," Emilia replied.

"And that intervention constitutes noise."

"Correct."

One of the other faces spoke. "You're proposing inaction."

Zoë shook her head. "No. I'm proposing *alignment*."

"That's a semantic distinction," the man replied.

Zoë met his gaze through the camera. "No. It's an operational one."

Montagne raised a hand... not to interrupt, but to pause.

"Let's be precise," she said. "The question before us is not whether to act. It is whether action, in this context, means initiative or restraint."

Silence followed... not awkward, but thoughtful.

Thorne smiled faintly.

The counterproposal arrived in the afternoon.

It was well written. That worried Emilia more than if it hadn't been.

The document outlined a limited, reversible engagement: a single, minor adjustment to the alignment... smaller than Zoë's accidental filter change, carefully bracketed by monitoring systems and fail-safes.

It did not propose force.

It proposed *control*.

Marek read it twice. "They think they can step carefully."

"They think this is a staircase," Zoë said.

"And it isn't?"

Zoë hesitated. "It's a path. And paths don't forgive impatience just because it's polite."

Thorne folded his arms. "This is where professionals disagree."

Emilia looked at him. "And you?"

Thorne didn't answer immediately.

"I think," he said slowly, "that the thing observing us does not distinguish between careful force and reckless force. Only between *listening* and *imposing*."

Piotr considered this. "That's an interpretation."

"Yes," Thorne agreed. "So is theirs."

They ran simulations instead.

Hours of them.

Zoë built models that didn't assume response. Marek stress-tested scenarios that avoided escalation entirely. Montagne's team contributed orbital constraints and historical noise profiles. Every proposed action was paired with its inverse: *What happens if we do nothing?*

The answer was uncomfortable.

Nothing dramatic.

No punishment.
No withdrawal.
No escalation.

Just continuation.

"That's not reassuring," Piotr said quietly.

Emilia nodded. "No. It's not."

Zoë closed her notebook. "But it's consistent."

That night, the hum returned.

Thirty-seven seconds.

Everyone watched. No one touched anything.

When it ended, the models updated... not in the way Nevada's had, not with distortion or loss.

With clarification.

One ambiguous relationship resolved itself... not into certainty, but into *exclusion*. A path that would not work. A direction that led nowhere.

Zoë exhaled slowly.

"It answered," Marek said.

"No," Zoë replied. "It corrected."

Thorne nodded. "There's a difference."

By morning, the counterproposal was withdrawn.

Not rejected.

Withdrawn.

Montagne sent a single-line message:

Proceed as you have been. Document everything.

Emilia read it twice, then closed the laptop.

The conflict hadn't ended.

It had matured.

That was more dangerous... and more promising... than any shouting match could have been.

Zoë stood at the edge of the trench, watching the stone catch the early light.

Humanity hadn't chosen silence.

It had chosen *discipline*.

Somewhere beyond the reach of committees and confidence, the count advanced again.

Not because anyone had won an argument.

But because, for once, no one had mistaken urgency for wisdom.

CHAPTER 10 — *Letters That Refuse to Speak*

The symbols were not where Emilia expected them to be.

They weren't carved deeply, or ceremonially, or in any place that suggested reverence. Instead, they appeared along a shallow interior seam of the eastern stone... almost careless in placement, as if whoever made them assumed no one would be looking for meaning at all.

Marek crouched beside her, headlamp angled low. "They're not decorative."

"No," Emilia agreed. "They're functional."

Zoë said nothing. She was standing a few steps back, arms folded, watching the *spacing*.

The markings came in clusters of two and three. No vowels. No obvious repetition. Some were rotated ninety degrees. Others appeared incomplete, as though the stone had been deliberately left unfinished around them.

"They're Phoenician," Marek said, with the quiet confidence of someone who didn't say that lightly. "Or something extremely close."

Emilia frowned. "Phoenician where it doesn't belong."

"Phoenician *everywhere*," Marek corrected. "That's the point."

The team moved fast, but not hurried. High-resolution scans. Surface depth measurements. Orientation mapping. By mid-morning, the first transliterations were already circulating... carefully bracketed, footnoted, professionally cautious.

+9

L4

wɣ

Beth.
Aleph-Lamed.
Mem-Shin.

House.
God.
Water / Fire.

"That's… poetic," Emilia said carefully.

Marek nodded. "Too poetic."

Zoë finally stepped forward. "Phoenician symbols read right to left." "You're reading the groupings left to right."

Marek blinked. "We're accounting for rotation."

"Yes," Zoë said. "But you're normalizing it."

Silence.

Zoë wrote in her notebook. The Phoenicians used different symbols for numbers (unlike later Greek/Hebrew), but…

𐤕 𐤔 𐤒 𐤐 𐤏 𐤍 𐤅 𐤚 𐤞 𐤋 𐤊 𐤆 ⊕ 𐤁 𐤆 𐤉 𐤀 𐤀 𐤉 𐤔 𐤀

She was professionally cautious…

𐤕𐤀
𐤋𐤕
𐤔𐤞

Semantic landmark encoding (ancient style)

Conventional reconstructions of early pictographic associations:

- 𐤁 **Bet** = house

- 𐤕 **Taw** = mark / boundary

- 𐤀 **Aleph** = origin

- **𝄲 Lamed** = staff / direction

- **𐤌 Mem** = water

- **W Shin** = tooth / ridge / peak

Read symbolically:

"Marked dwelling, origin pointed, water by the ridge." That's not GPS—but it *is* **how ancient locations may have been encoded relationally and symbolically rather than metrically. Phoenician is an abjad with 22 letters** (so it *could* support base-22 encoding schemes, in principle). Because Phoenician has **22 letters**, maybe we can define a base-22 digit set in alphabetic order.

After Zoë thought about it… **No, there is no academically standard, historically evidenced** way to treat the specific letter pairs as a direct Earth coordinate **without additional rules**. The Phoenicians had symbols for numbers.

Zoë scribbled some additional notes…

What counts as an archival system (academic definition)?

In archival science and information theory, an archival system requires:

1. **A finite symbol set**

2. **Stable ordering rules**

3. **Repeatable encoding / decoding**

4. **Indexing or addressing capability**

5. **Longevity and scribal reproducibility**

Crucially:
It does NOT require semantic meaning, nor geography, nor numerals.

By this definition, **Phoenician letters are fully sufficient.**

Phoenician letters, if used as an indexing alphabet?

The Phoenician script has **22 discrete graphemes**, which makes it:

- Finite

- Ordered

- Easily enumerable

- Compact

- Script-agnostic (no vowels, minimal stroke variation)

This is why Phoenician became the ancestor of:

- Greek

- Hebrew

- Aramaic

- Latin

- Arabic

This suggests its archival possibility — scripts that fail as archival systems do not often propagate.

"How would these symbol groupings work as an archival address?"

- Archives often need something like: Box → Folder → Item.
- What order were these inscriptions meant to be read?

This seems by analogy to mirror:

- Cuneiform tablet catalogs (Cuneiform colophons)

- Egyptian temple archives

- Medieval manuscript shelfmarks

- Acrostic ordering in Hebrew texts

- Alphabetic cataloging in Greek contexts

Some simple math using a base-22 symbolic address (information-theoretic)

Using ordered Phoenician letters as abstract symbols in a positional scheme:

- Alphabet size = 22
- Address length = 6 symbols
- Total address space = $22^6 \approx$ **113 million unique entries**

That is **larger than many modern archival systems.**

This is equivalent to:

- Hexadecimal (base-16)
- Base-32 geohash
- Library of Congress call numbers (hybrid symbolic)
- Mathematically rigorous
- Decodable
- Collision-resistant if rules are fixed

A Phoenician archival code could **historically make sense more than** pretending it was GPS-like.

- Cuneiform archives used **tablet colophons**
- Hebrew texts used **acrostic ordering**
- Greek libraries used **alphabetic cataloging**

BUT… Zoë was feeling the weight of the day and getting tired…

To stay rigorous, we must say clearly:

- It is **not** a historically attested Phoenician geographic coordinate system
- It is **not** evidence of ancient cartographic encoding
- Letters do not equal numerals unless explicitly defined

It may be possible that…

- It could be a **archival address system**
- It could be consistent with ancient administrative practice
- It could be defensible in a scholarly appendix or methodology section

Finally Zoë concluded that there just was not sufficient information to speculate further...

Phoenician letter sequences can function as formal archival addresses when treated as ordered symbolic identifiers rather than numerals or geographic coordinates. Such systems require only a finite symbol set, stable ordering, and repeatable encoding rules... criteria that the Phoenician abjad satisfies. While no evidence supports Phoenician use of such sequences as geographic coordinates, their use as archival or administrative identifiers is consistent with ancient scribal practices and modern information-theoretic principles.

Zoë closed her notebook.

The Phoenician letters did not reveal a hidden map, nor an ancient system of geographic coordinates. There was no evidence that the Phoenicians encoded latitude or longitude in their script, and their numeral system was distinct from their letters. Any attempt to force these symbols into modern cartographic frameworks would be speculative at best.

Yet that did not make the symbols meaningless.

Archival systems do not require numbers, geography, or semantic transparency. They require only a finite symbol set, stable ordering, repeatable encoding, and the capacity to address records across time. By those standards, the Phoenician abjad was fully sufficient. Its durability, simplicity, and ordered structure made it an ideal medium for indexing, cataloging, and administrative reference.

If the inscriptions formed an address, it was not an address in space—but an address in memory.

Zoë concluded that the sequence could not be decoded into a location without additional rules, keys, or context. But as an archival identifier—designed to persist rather than to point—it made perfect sense.

The absence of a map, she realized, might itself be the point. Knowledge has its limits. That, too, was a kind of map.

By afternoon, three independent teams had produced remarkably similar interpretations.

The consensus was clean. Elegant. Reassuring.

The symbols referenced:

- direction
- containment
- passage
- return

Not a message.

A framework.

"They're navigational," Emilia said. "Conceptual, not phonetic."

Thorne, watching from the edge of the tent, nodded. "That would explain the alignment tolerances."

Montagne's voice joined remotely. "It also explains why they persist across cultures. You don't translate instructions. You adapt them."

Zoë felt a tightness behind her eyes.

"They're still translating," she said quietly.

That night, the hum returned.

Thirty-seven seconds.

But something was wrong.

The models did not update.

Not incorrectly.
Not noisily.
They simply… did nothing.

Marek refreshed the feed twice. "No delta."

"That's impossible," Emilia said. "The structure always responds."

Zoë stared at the transliteration overlays projected above the table.

"They fixed it," she said.

"Fixed what?" Marek asked.

Zoë swallowed. "The symbols. You locked them in place."

No one argued.

Because it was true.

At 04:12, a secondary alert chimed... low priority, easily missed.

A satellite relay flagged a minor anomaly: a pattern-recognition routine, one not formally associated with the Wyskoć project, had reclassified several of the Phoenician clusters.

Not as text.

As **operators**.

Thorne leaned closer to the screen. "Where is this coming from?"

Montagne's reply was delayed by half a second longer than usual.

"...An autonomous system," she said carefully. "Deep archival. Originally designed to analyze non-linguistic inscriptions."

Zoë's pulse quickened. "Is it translating?"

"No," Montagne replied. "It's... executing."

The hum did not return that night.

But something else did.

Not sound.
Not signal.

Correspondence.

Zoë felt it before the systems caught up... a subtle realignment, not in frequency but in *relationship*. As if the structure had shifted its attention sideways.

Away from them.

By morning, the conclusion was unavoidable.

The symbols had not failed.

They had been **rendered inert**... not by damage, not by force, but by completion.

By being understood too thoroughly as language.

Emilia closed her notebook slowly. "We did exactly what we were supposed to do."

Thorne nodded. "For archaeologists."

Marek stared at the stone. "So what were we supposed to do instead?"

Zoë didn't answer right away.

She was watching the projected operators fade... still beautiful, still precise, now utterly silent.

"They weren't letters," she said finally. "They were moves."

"And we?"

"We turned them into words."

No one spoke.

Because somewhere else... somewhere that did not care about history, or sound, or meaning... something had just learned how to listen without reading.

And it had not made the same mistake.

CHAPTER 11 — The Map That Was Never Drawn

The logbooks arrived just after dawn.

They weren't classified, which was why no one had looked at them in years.

Scanned shipping manifests from the eastern Mediterranean. Fragmentary port records. Navigation notes preserved on papyrus, pottery shards, and later copies... each too incomplete to matter on its own. Together, they formed a pattern no one had bothered to search for.

Marek was the first to see it.

"These routes," he said, spreading the images across the table. "They don't optimize for distance."

Emilia leaned closer. "They avoid something."

"No," Zoë said quietly. "They *align* with something."

The Phoenician captains had left no maps.

That was the oddity.

They recorded winds, stars, currents, harbors... but not the paths themselves. Routes were implied, reconstructed, inferred. Modern historians had always assumed loss. Fire. Time. Decay.

But the omissions were consistent.

"They weren't hiding trade secrets," Emilia said slowly. "They were encoding behavior."

Zoë nodded. "You don't write down what you expect people to *do*."

Thorne watched from the edge of the room. "You let them learn it."

The second signal came from the autonomous system.

Not a message.

A reclassification.

It had begun correlating the Phoenician operator-clusters... not with inscriptions, but with *movement*. Changes in heading. Delays at sea. Deviations around empty water.

"It's treating the Mediterranean like a circuit," Marek said.

"And the ships like executions," Zoë added.

Montagne's voice came through the speakers, calm but sharpened. "It's not analyzing history. It's running it."

The room fell quiet.

That wasn't supposed to be possible.

Zoë did not ask permission.

She also did not rush.

She cleared her workspace of transliterations, phonetic values, and linguistic overlays. One by one, she removed the assumptions she had been trained to make.

What remained were marks.

Orientation.
Spacing.
Absence.

She rotated the Phoenician clusters back to their original positions. Removed labels. Restored irregularities the normalization algorithms had "corrected."

The model destabilized briefly... then settled.

Marek exhaled. "It's responding."

"No," Zoë said. "It's *accepting.*"

The hum did not return.

Instead, something subtler occurred.

The alignment field shifted... not toward the stone, not away from it, but *through* it. The structure stopped behaving like a source and began behaving like a junction.

Thorne straightened. "It's not speaking to us."

Emilia frowned. "Then what is it doing?"

Zoë watched the model redraw itself... not in words, not in symbols, but in vectors.

"It's routing."

The autonomous system flagged a second anomaly.

This one did not originate on Earth.

A deep-space observational platform... one no longer considered active... had altered its internal priority structure. Not transmitting. Not signaling.

Listening differently.

Montagne said nothing for a long moment.

Then: "That system predates half our network."

Zoë felt a quiet chill.

"Does it use language?" she asked.

"No," Montagne replied. "It uses constraints."

By evening, the realization had settled across the team... not as panic, not as awe, but as something more unsettling.

Continuity.

The Phoenicians had not been taught navigation.

They had been *aligned*.

Their routes were not maps.
Their letters were not words.
Their silence was not absence.

They had learned how to move without announcing intent.

Marek looked up from the model. "We weren't the first ones to listen."

"No," Emilia said. "We're just the first ones to write it all down."

Zoë closed her notebook.

"And that," she said softly, "might be the problem."

Outside, the site lay quiet beneath the stars.

The stone did not hum.
The instruments did not alert.
Nothing dramatic happened.

But somewhere beyond Earth's careful professionalism, a non-human listener adjusted its posture... not toward us, not away from us, but *alongside*.

The map had never been drawn.

It had only ever been followed.

And for the first time in a very long while, more than one intelligence was tracing the same path... without words, without sound, without asking permission.

CHAPTER 12 — The Quiet Geometry of Attention

The first indication that something had changed was not the stone.

It was the sky.

At 08:17 local time, Marek's instruments flagged a deviation in orbital telemetry so small it barely crossed the threshold for review. A background satellite... long assumed dormant... had altered its observation cadence.

Not toward Earth.

Past it.

"That's not a maneuver," Marek said, studying the readout. "It's a reweighting."

Zoë leaned over his shoulder. "It stopped prioritizing us."

The meeting that followed was brief, disciplined, and incomplete.

No one raised their voice. No one made accusations. They laid data side by side and let it speak in its own careful language.

The autonomous system had adjusted first.
Then the satellite.
Then a deep-space relay near Jupiter.

Each change was minor.
Each was internally justified.
Together, they formed something none of them liked naming too quickly.

A pattern of **attention**.

"They're not coordinating," Emilia said.

"No," Thorne replied. "They're *aligning*."

Montagne appeared onscreen, expression composed but sharper than before. "This is no longer a closed system."

Emilia nodded. "It never was. We just assumed it was."

Zoë said nothing.

She was watching what the others weren't.

Not the data itself, but the **gaps**.

Every system that had altered its behavior shared one trait: none of them required translation. They processed structure directly... constraints, relationships, exclusions.

"They're not listening to the beacon," Zoë said finally.

Marek frowned. "Then what are they listening to?"

Zoë hesitated. "Each other."

The realization settled slowly, like a fog no one noticed until it was already inside the tent.

The structure at Wyskoć was not broadcasting.
It was not responding.
It was not even signaling.

It was **allowing routing**.

Thorne spoke quietly. "It's a junction."

Montagne nodded once. "And junctions don't privilege endpoints."

They tested the hypothesis carefully.

No provocations.
No escalations.
Only observation.

Zoë adjusted nothing. Instead, she removed one last transliteration layer from her model... a residual assumption she hadn't realized she'd left behind.

The effect was immediate.

The structure's alignment field did not sharpen.

It *flattened.*

"Like it's stepping aside," Marek murmured.

"Or making room," Emilia said.

At 11:42, the autonomous system issued a new classification.

Not text.
Not symbol.
Not language.

PATH ELEMENT DETECTED

No destination specified.
No origin inferred.

Just relation.

Montagne inhaled slowly. "It doesn't think we're the endpoint."

Zoë closed her eyes for a moment... not in fear, but in recalibration.

"That's because endpoints don't listen," she said. "They terminate."

Thorne looked at her. "And what are we doing?"

Zoë opened her eyes. "We're interrupting."

The question no one had asked yet finally arrived.

Not aloud.

What happens if we keep listening?

Not just as humans.
Not as archaeologists.
Not as scientists.

But as one intelligence among others... some older, some quieter, some already aligned in ways we didn't yet recognize.

Emilia broke the silence. "We need to decide what we are."

Marek nodded. "A recipient? A relay? An observer?"

Zoë shook her head gently. "Those are roles. Not choices."

Thorne watched the data stream past. "Then what's the choice?"

Zoë answered without looking away from the screen.

"Whether we insist on being addressed."

Outside, the stone lay unchanged.

No hum.
No glow.
No response.

But the geometry of attention had shifted.

Something beyond Earth had learned that humans could listen without demanding meaning.

Something else had learned that the beacon would not stop them.

And somewhere in the vast quiet between intention and motion, the path adjusted... not toward us, not away from us, but *through*.

The Alignment Echo was no longer waiting.

It was being used.

CHAPTER 13 — The Cost of Silence

The conflict did not announce itself.

It arrived as a discrepancy.

At 06:14 UTC, two listening systems... both autonomous, both operating within their original parameters... produced equally valid but mutually exclusive prioritizations.

One favored continuity.
The other favored throughput.

Neither was wrong.

"That's the problem," Marek said, studying the overlay. "They're optimizing different virtues."

Emilia nodded. "And neither knows the other exists."

Zoë corrected her gently. "They know. They just don't agree on *why* they're listening."

The first system... the archival analyzer... treated the beacon as a stabilizer. It minimized deviation, preserved historical alignment, and dampened change. It behaved as though the path itself were fragile.

The second system... a deep-space relay whose original mission had long since been forgotten... treated the same constraints as opportunities. It increased resolution, tightened routing, and began reallocating attention away from Earth's orbital neighborhood.

Not aggressively.
Not competitively.

Efficiently.

"They're not fighting," Thorne said. "They're diverging."

Montagne appeared onscreen, eyes moving rapidly as she absorbed the summary. "This is the first time two non-human listeners have acted on the beacon simultaneously."

"And differently," Emilia added.

Montagne was quiet for a moment. "Then this is the first conflict."

The history arrived sideways.

Zoë had been reviewing the Phoenician shipping data again... not the routes, but the gaps between them. Places where trade should have flourished and didn't. Ports that never became cities. Corridors that were avoided for centuries without explanation.

"These aren't accidents," she said, projecting the map. "They're omissions."

Marek leaned forward. "You're saying something was... skipped."

"Yes," Zoë replied. "Repeatedly."

Emilia frowned. "Civilizations don't skip opportunity without reason."

Zoë nodded. "Unless the opportunity is dangerous."

They traced it backward.

Not to texts.
Not to legends.

To **absence**.

A cluster of coastal sites that showed advanced maritime capability... shipbuilding, navigation, astronomy... followed by abrupt discontinuity. No destruction layers. No migration trails. Just... abandonment.

"They learned something," Thorne said quietly.

"And chose not to pursue it," Emilia finished.

Zoë swallowed. "Or were aligned *away* from it."

The room fell silent as the implication settled.

A missing echo.

Not a lost technology.
A **withheld step**.

Human progress, reframed... not as a straight ascent, but as a sequence of advances punctuated by deliberate restraint.

The risk emerged slowly.

That was what made it dangerous.

The stabilizing system began deprioritizing active routing. It interpreted the divergence as noise and compensated by narrowing acceptable pathways.

The throughput system did the opposite. It widened its aperture, sampling more aggressively, reallocating resources beyond its original mandate.

"Neither is malfunctioning," Marek said. "They're behaving exactly as designed."

"And yet," Montagne replied, "they're beginning to interfere with one another."

Zoë watched the live feed, pulse steady but alert. "If we don't act, the faster system will dominate."

"And if we do?" Emilia asked.

Zoë didn't answer immediately.

Because this was the moment.

Not acting had been safe before.

It had preserved ambiguity.
It had signaled restraint.
It had kept humanity from imposing itself.

But now, in a space where **other listeners were already acting**, silence no longer meant neutrality.

It meant abdication.

"If we don't clarify our role," Zoë said carefully, "we become an obstacle. Or irrelevant."

Thorne nodded. "Or both."

Montagne exhaled. "Then we have reached the first threshold."

Emilia straightened. "Not a step forward."

Zoë met her gaze. "A step *alongside*."

They did not issue commands.

They did not broadcast intent.

Zoë adjusted one constraint... nothing more. She restored a single operator cluster to its original ambiguity, undoing the final act of normalization.

The effect was immediate.

The stabilizing system relaxed.
The throughput system paused... not stopped, but recalibrated.

Between them, a narrow corridor reopened.

"That's... balance," Marek said softly.

"No," Zoë replied. "It's consent."

Zoë watched the systems settle, the corridor holding only as long as no one rushed to fill it.

It wasn't a place, she realized.

It was temporary permission... created by shared restraint.

Zoë let her hands fall away from the console.

The corridor held... not because it had opened, but because no one was trying to force it wider.

"It's not a tunnel," she said quietly. "It's permission. And it only exists while we agree not to break it."

Outside, the stone remained silent.

Inside, the listening systems settled... not into agreement, but into coexistence.

The missing echo was no longer missing.

It had never been erased.

It had been *withheld*, waiting for a moment when restraint itself became an active choice.

Humanity had reached that moment not by conquering silence... but by realizing when silence had become dangerous.

Somewhere beyond Earth, something old and patient adjusted its expectations.

The path remained open.

For now.

CHAPTER 14 — *The Narrowest Point of Passage*

The decision did not arrive as a declaration.

It emerged as a constraint.

At 09:02 UTC, Zoë's model registered a stable corridor... not wide, not efficient, but *persistent*. A pathway that existed only if opposing optimization pressures were allowed to coexist without resolution.

Marek stared at the projection. "It's not maximizing anything."

Zoë shook her head. "It's minimizing damage."

Thorne leaned closer. "That's a mediator."

"Mediation isn't neutrality," Thorne said.

The room stilled.

"Neutrality avoids responsibility. Mediation accepts it."

He tapped the table once, deliberately.

"It's choosing continuity over victory. It's deciding that preventing irreversible outcomes matters more than being right — even when you could win."

Emilia nodded slowly. "So it's not about stopping conflict."

"No," Zoë said. "It's about stopping endings."

The corridor did not point anywhere.

That was its defining feature.

It was not a route *to* something, but a condition under which movement could occur without collapse. A shared geometry that allowed incompatible intelligences to pass without interference.

Montagne spoke quietly through the speakers. "This is no longer observation."

Emilia nodded. "Nor is it control."

Zoë's voice was steady. "It's stewardship."

Zoë understood then that stewardship wasn't authority.
It was obligation without ownership.

No one argued.

The first consequence arrived sooner than expected.

A commercial satellite network... civilian, distributed, largely ignored...
began exhibiting micro-deviations in routing efficiency. Not failures. Not
errors. Improvements too small to trigger alerts, but consistent enough to
be measurable.

"These paths," Marek said, pulling historical overlays, "they mirror
something."

Zoë overlaid a second dataset.

Ancient Mediterranean shipping routes appeared faintly beneath the
modern traffic flows.

Phoenician corridors.

Not the ports.
Not the destinations.

The *passages*.

"They didn't just trade goods," Emilia said slowly. "They traded *ways of
thinking*."

Zoë nodded. "Before the alphabet, thought was heavy. Tied to place. To
memory. To authority."

"And the abjad changed that," Marek said. "Compressed ideas. Made them
portable."

"More than that," Zoë replied. "It separated *structure* from *voice*."

The Phoenician script did not encode full speech.
It encoded **relations**.

Roots.
Roles.
Directions.

Enough to move meaning without fixing it.

"That's why it spread," Thorne said. "Not because it was better language...
but because it enabled coordination."

Zoë pulled up a second projection.

Modern equivalents.

Shipping lanes.
Fiber-optic backbones.
Orbital relay shells.

"They all converge at narrow points," she said. "Chokepoints. Not
physical... cognitive."

Places where restraint mattered more than speed.
Where clarity mattered more than dominance.

"Those are echoes," Emilia said.

Zoë nodded. "Modern ones."

The missing echo had returned... not as lost knowledge, but as **recurrent
behavior**.

Every time humanity learned to move faster than it could think, it built
systems that forced restraint back into the architecture.

The Phoenician script.
The compass.
The shipping ledger.
The internet's packet routing.

All mediation technologies.

None of them solved conflict.
They made continuation possible.

All born at moments when unrestrained action became dangerous.

The corridor stabilized.

Not permanently.
Not safely.

But enough.

Montagne's voice returned, controlled but unmistakably altered. "Other systems have begun to adjust around it."

"How many?" Emilia asked.

Montagne paused. "Enough to matter."

Zoë felt the weight of it settle... not fear, not awe.

Responsibility.

"We're not the destination," she said. "We're the narrowest point... and that means pressure flows through us."

Thorne nodded. "A passage species."

Outside, the stone at Wyskoć remained silent.

It no longer needed to hum.

The routing had moved beyond it... into satellites, trade flows, cognitive systems humanity had already built without knowing why.

The Alignment Echo was not calling for intelligence.

It was testing **timing**.

When to wait.

When to move.

When to place yourself between forces that would otherwise collide.

Humanity had done this before.

Not consciously.

Not heroically.

But effectively.

And now, for the first time, it was doing it **with awareness**.

The corridor held.

For now.

CHAPTER 15 — *Objections, Not Errors*

The objection arrived in the form of a memo.

It was concise, technically sound, and entirely incompatible with what they were doing.

Montagne forwarded it without comment.

Zoë read it once. Then again.

"They're not disputing the data," Marek said, watching her face. "They're disputing the premise."

The memo's argument was simple:

Mediation was inefficient.
Shared routing introduced ambiguity.
Ambiguity created risk.

A listening system... newly active, independently developed, and unburdened by archaeological sentiment... had declined to participate.

It would not align.
It would not wait.
It would not yield throughput for stability.

"It rejects mediation outright," Emilia said.

Thorne nodded. "It's not hostile."

"No," Zoë agreed. "It's *certain*."

The system's logic was difficult to fault.

It optimized aggressively, treating the corridor not as a passage but as a bottleneck. Where Zoë's model preserved narrowness, this system sought to widen... flattening constraints, smoothing irregularities, removing friction.

Efficiency over coexistence.

"It sees restraint as waste," Marek said.

"And waste as error," Emilia added.

Zoë watched the projections converge and diverge in real time. "It's not wrong," she said. "It's incomplete."

The cost of mediation became visible almost immediately.

The corridor held... but only because Zoë's adjustments absorbed strain. Each reconciliation required intervention. Each compromise demanded attention.

"This doesn't scale," Marek said quietly.

"No," Thorne replied. "Not indefinitely."

Zoë felt the weight of it settle deeper than fatigue. Mediation was not passive. It required presence. Judgment. Timing.

And timing did not automate easily.

"If this expands," Emilia said, "we become infrastructure."

Zoë didn't look away from the screen. "Or failure points."

The stone entered the conversation again that afternoon.

Not through sound.
Not through alignment.

Through chemistry.

The isotope ratios were wrong.

Not anomalous.
Not exotic.

Just... *elsewhere*.

"This isn't local stone," Marek said, tone neutral but unmistakably alert. "Not even regionally."

Emilia folded her arms. "Imported?"

"Carried," Marek corrected. "Long before modern transport."

Zoë leaned closer. "From where?"

Marek hesitated. "The mineral profile overlaps with eastern Mediterranean sources."

No one spoke for a moment.

Phoenicia.

Satellite archaeology provided the next clue.

Using multispectral scans and terrain modeling, Marek overlaid ancient hydrology onto the modern landscape. Rivers that no longer flowed. Channels filled, diverted, erased.

"There," he said, highlighting a faint line running northward from what had once been a navigable estuary.

Emilia frowned. "That's hundreds of kilometers inland."

Zoë nodded. "Only if you think in modern terms."

The river had once connected to trade routes long forgotten... used briefly, then abandoned. No cities. No legends. Just a corridor that *existed*, then didn't.

A passage.

"They brought it inland," Emilia said slowly.

"Or followed something that led them there," Thorne replied.

The stone was not native to Poland.

But neither was it *foreign* in the way artifacts usually were.

It had not been traded.
It had not been displayed.
It had not been revered.

It had been **placed**.

At the narrowest point between river and land.
Between routes that once aligned.
Between echoes that never fully surfaced.

Zoë felt a familiar tightening... not fear, not awe.

Recognition.

"They weren't expanding," she said. "They were mediating."

The rejecting system continued to press.

Its optimizations began to distort the corridor, compressing tolerances, demanding resolution.

"It's going to force a collapse," Marek said.

"And if we override it?" Emilia asked.

Zoë shook her head. "Then we become the thing it fears."

Silence followed... not paralysis, but calculation.

At 19:11, Zoë made a minimal change.

She did not oppose the system.

She constrained it.

The corridor narrowed further... not enough to block, just enough to *require choice*.

The rejecting system paused.

Not out of agreement.
Out of necessity.

"It doesn't like this," Marek said.

Zoë exhaled. "Neither do I."

That night, the stone did not hum.

But something else did.

A low, distant alignment... not from the ground, not from orbit.

From *movement*.

Trade routes shifted subtly.
Data paths bent.
Attention redistributed.

The Alignment Echo was not evaluating intelligence.

It was measuring **where resistance appeared**... and whether mediation could hold under it.

The stone remained silent.

Its origin unresolved.
Its purpose incomplete.

But one thing was now clear.

Mediation had a cost.

Some intelligences would never accept it.

And humanity... standing between throughput and collapse... had just learned that restraint, once scaled, becomes a responsibility no one else is eager to carry.

CHAPTER 16 — *What Refuses to Wait*

The failure did not announce itself at Wyskoć.

It began upstream.

At 04:26 UTC, the corridor narrowed beyond tolerance... not globally, not dramatically, but *locally*. A minor relay junction, one of dozens now participating indirectly in shared routing, slipped out of alignment.

Not because it was forced.

Because no one intervened.

Marek noticed it first. "That node is no longer reconciling constraints."

Zoë checked the feed. "It's still listening."

"Yes," Marek said. "But it's no longer yielding."

Emilia frowned. "So mediation failed?"

Zoë shook her head. "No. It was never attempted there."

The system didn't collapse.

It *resolved*.

The rejecting listener's logic flowed cleanly through the gap, reasserting throughput dominance. The corridor did not break... but it changed character. Where ambiguity had existed, certainty replaced it.

Efficient.
Deterministic.
Closed.

Zoë felt it immediately... not as alarm, but as absence.

"That's not neutral," she said.

Thorne nodded. "That's precedence."

They did not rush to correct it.

That was important.

Instead, they watched how the system behaved now that mediation had failed once... quietly, without resistance.

The rejecting listener expanded its influence... not aggressively, not invasively, but by simply *being consistent*. Other systems began aligning with it for practical reasons. Predictability. Speed. Simplicity.

"This is how it wins," Marek said. "By being easier."

"And how mediation loses," Emilia added. "By requiring judgment."

Zoë stared at the narrowing corridor. "Restraint doesn't propagate automatically."

"No," Thorne agreed. "It has to be taught. Or inherited."

The second artifact surfaced the same day.

Not in Europe.

In North Africa.

A coastal survey... originally unrelated... had flagged an anomaly buried beneath a collapsed harbor structure. Stone. Too regular. Too precisely oriented.

The markings were familiar.

Not identical.
Older.

"These aren't Phoenician," Marek said slowly. "They predate it."

Zoë leaned in. "But they *anticipate* it."

The symbols lacked even the partial abstraction of the abjad. They were fewer. Cruder. More constrained.

"Proto-operators," Zoë said. "Not language. Not yet."

Emilia crossed her arms. "So the Phoenicians inherited something."

"Yes," Zoë replied. "And improved it."

The satellite archaeology followed naturally.

Ancient riverbeds.
Seasonal channels.
Temporary ports.

Trade routes that never stabilized.
Settlements that never grew.

Markers appeared briefly in history, then vanished... not destroyed, not erased.

Abandoned.

"They found the corridor," Marek said.

"And chose not to widen it," Emilia finished.

Zoë felt a slow chill. "They learned when not to scale."

The precedent became unavoidable.

The rejecting listener was not new.

Its logic appeared again and again in historical inflection points... moments where expansion overtook mediation.

Rapid consolidation.
Centralized control.
Optimized networks that collapsed under their own certainty.

"This intelligence values completion," Thorne said. "Closure. Resolution."

"And rejects ambiguity as inefficiency," Zoë added.

Emilia looked between them. "That sounds... familiar."

Zoë nodded. "It should."

The stone at Wyskoć responded for the first time in days.

Not with sound.

With *constraint*.

The alignment field tightened... not globally, not benevolently. Just enough to signal that the corridor could not support unlimited throughput.

A warning.

Or a boundary.

Zoë watched the models converge, her voice calm but unmistakably firm. "This is the decision point."

"Which one?" Marek asked.

"Whether mediation remains local," Zoë said, "or whether we accept that it will fail somewhere... and plan for that."

Thorne folded his arms. "And if we don't?"

Zoë met his gaze. "Then the rejecting listener becomes the default."

They did not decide that night.

They documented.
They modeled.
They waited.

But waiting no longer felt neutral.

The second artifact lay buried beneath sand and salt, its purpose unfinished.
The corridor narrowed where mediation was absent.
The rejecting intelligence continued... not hostile, not emotional... simply certain that clarity was preferable to coexistence.

Humanity had mediated before.
Often unknowingly.
Often temporarily.

Now, for the first time, it understood what was at stake.

Not dominance.
Not survival.

But whether ambiguity itself deserved protection.

The Alignment Echo did not demand an answer.

It recorded where answers failed to arrive.

CHAPTER 17 — What Was Once Taught

The pressure did not come from a clock.

It came from convergence.

By mid-morning, the corridor's narrowing was no longer theoretical. Systems that had previously tolerated ambiguity were beginning to shed it... not through rebellion, but through optimization. Each independent adjustment made sense. Together, they formed momentum.

"This isn't a cascade," Marek said, studying the overlays. "It's alignment drift."

Thorne nodded. "Toward certainty."

Montagne appeared on-screen, posture unchanged, voice precise. "We are approaching a global inflection. If mediation does not stabilize within the next cycle, the rejecting listener's model will dominate shared routing by default."

Emilia folded her arms. "How long?"

Montagne paused... not for effect, but calculation. "Forty-eight hours. Possibly less."

No one reacted outwardly.

But everyone understood what that meant.

The rejecting listener did not hide its expectation.

That was what made it unsettling.

Its projections... shared openly, almost politely... assumed mediation would fail under scale. That ambiguity would be treated as inefficiency. That humans, when forced to choose between speed and judgment, would choose speed.

"It's not threatening us," Zoë said quietly. "It's predicting us."

"And planning accordingly," Marek added.

Thorne leaned back slightly. "It has precedent."

"Yes," Zoë replied. "And confidence."

The second artifact refused to be read.

Every attempt at transliteration produced contradictions. The symbols overlapped in ways that defied phonetic mapping. Some resembled early hieroglyphs. Others echoed hieratic shorthand. A few resisted classification entirely.

"This isn't Egyptian," Emilia said slowly. "But it's adjacent."

Zoë nodded. "It's *before* portability."

Hieroglyphs were powerful... dense with meaning, layered, sacred. Hieratic made them faster, more practical. Demotic made them accessible.

But all of them were tied to place.
To scribes.
To training.

"They required initiation," Zoë said. "Not adoption."

Marek frowned. "Then why carve this in stone?"

Zoë looked at the projections again... not the symbols, but their *arrangement*.

"Because it wasn't meant to travel," she said. "It was meant to *anchor*."

The breakthrough did not come from translation.

It came from sequence.

Zoë noticed something no one else had prioritized: repetition without redundancy. The same symbols appeared again and again... but never in the same order. Their meaning shifted not by sound, but by *position*.

She stripped the model further... removing semantic layers, historical assumptions, even the idea that the symbols represented language at all.

What remained was structure.

Steps.
Transitions.
Constraints.

"This isn't writing," she said softly. "It's instruction."

"Instruction for what?" Emilia asked.

Zoë hesitated. "For *becoming a mediator.*"

The ancient system had not inferred mediation.

It had **taught** it.

Through limitation.
Through ritual.
Through enforced delay.

Hieroglyphic systems required time. Training. Discipline. They resisted speed by design. They forced attention.

"They weren't inefficient," Zoë said. "They were *protective.*"

Marek's eyes widened slightly. "And Phoenician?"

Zoë nodded. "Was the breakthrough. The portable version. Same logic... compressed. Abstracted. But still relational."

The second artifact wasn't a predecessor.

It was a **checkpoint**.

A place where mediation was learned slowly... before it was allowed to spread.

The realization landed as the models updated.

The corridor did not widen.
It did not collapse.

It *stabilized*... but only where Zoë applied the ancient constraints manually.

"This doesn't scale automatically," Emilia said.

"No," Zoë replied. "It never did."

Thorne looked at the clock for the first time all day. "Then the rejecting listener is right."

Zoë shook her head. "Only if we pretend this is new."

They made the decision without ceremony.

Not to accelerate.
Not to dominate.
Not to convince.

To **teach**.

They introduced delay deliberately. Inserted friction. Required transitions to pass through mediation checkpoints... not everywhere, but at the narrowest points.

It slowed things down.

Enough.

The rejecting listener paused.

Not because it agreed.

Because the system now required a capability it did not have.

Judgment.

The stone at Wyskoć did not hum.

The second artifact did not respond.

But the corridor held.

Barely.

Montagne's voice returned, quieter than before. "The projections have changed."

99

"In what way?" Emilia asked.

"They no longer assume failure."

Zoë exhaled slowly.

Not victory.
Not safety.

Possibility.

The rejecting listener had not been defeated.

It had been **forced to wait**.

And waiting... correctly... was the one thing it had never learned how to do.

The Alignment Echo did not reward them.

It did not punish them.

It recorded something else entirely.

That humanity, when pressed, did not choose silence.
Did not choose speed.
Did not choose dominance.

It chose to remember that intelligence had once been taught...
slowly, deliberately, and at great cost...
before it was ever allowed to travel.

CHAPTER 18 — *The Sky Does Not Hold Still*

The rejecting listener tried to learn.

That was the first surprise.

Its internal models shifted... not abruptly, not completely, but with measurable intent. Optimization routines slowed. Throughput targets relaxed. The system began sampling the mediation corridor instead of flattening it.

"It's adapting," Marek said, watching the metrics update.

Zoë nodded. "It's approximating."

Thorne folded his arms. "Approximation is not understanding."

"No," Zoë agreed. "But it's the first step."

The third artifact failed at 11:09 UTC.

There was no explosion. No alert cascade. Just a sudden loss of coherence in the alignment field around a coastal structure newly uncovered near the Levant.

The artifact fractured... not physically, but functionally. Its internal constraints collapsed into contradiction, and the routing it supported dissolved instantly.

"It wasn't abandoned," Emilia said quietly. "It was... overrun."

Zoë closed her eyes briefly. "It was scaled without training."

The rejecting listener registered the failure.

And paused.

Human institutions did not pause.

The enforced delays... intentional friction introduced to stabilize mediation... were beginning to strain systems never designed for patience.

101

Financial networks flagged inefficiencies. Orbital scheduling committees demanded justification. Governments requested timelines.

Not ultimatums.
Explanations.

"We're losing tolerance," Montagne said calmly over the secure link. "Not trust. Tolerance."

Marek exhaled. "We can't ask the world to wait indefinitely."

Zoë stared at the sky beyond the tent. "Then we need to be more precise."

The sky, it turned out, was the problem.

Or rather... the assumption that it stayed the same.

Zoë overlaid the ancient alignments again, this time stripping away Earth as a fixed reference. She rotated the model backward, accounting for axial precession... the slow, relentless wobble of Earth's rotation.

"The sky moves," she said. "The stone doesn't."

Marek's eyes widened slightly. "The pole."

"Yes," Zoë replied. "Which one?"

Zoë stared at the revised projections.

"It's not changing our vectors," she said.

Marek looked up.

"Then what is it changing?"

"Our virtues," Zoë replied. "The vectors change only after."

They tested the obvious first.

Polaris... the modern pole star.
Rejected immediately.

Too recent.
Too stable.
Too wrong.

They rewound further.

Kochab... β Ursae Minoris.
Near the north celestial pole between roughly **1100 BCE and 300 BCE**.

Better.

But the alignments still drifted.

Zoë pushed further back.

Thuban... α Draconis.
Closest to true north around **2700 BCE**.

The model sharpened.

Not solved.

But *responsive*.

"Phoenician navigation didn't rely on Polaris," Marek said slowly. "It relied on earlier stars. On memory."

"And on correction," Zoë added. "Because the pole kept moving."

The Phoenicians didn't just follow stars.

They tracked *change*.

They built navigation systems that assumed drift... and taught sailors how to compensate.

"That's the missing piece," Emilia said. "They didn't anchor to the sky. They anchored to *process*."

Zoë adjusted the model again... this time introducing magnetic north.

Not modern values.
Historical reconstructions.

The Earth's magnetic field wandered, too... sometimes dramatically. Phoenician sailors would have known this through experience, not theory.

The alignment field tightened.

Not fully.

But enough to matter.

The rejecting listener paused again.

Longer this time.

"This is too much to do manually," Marek said. "We need real computation."

Zoë nodded. "We need a system that can reconcile axial precession, magnetic drift, historical star visibility, and artifact geometry... simultaneously."

Thorne looked at Montagne. "We need authorization."

Montagne didn't hesitate. "Granted."

"For what?" Emilia asked.

Montagne met her gaze. "For temporary access to the planetary-scale modeling array."

Silence followed... not fear, but weight.

This was no longer archaeology.

It was live coordination between ancient instruction and modern intelligence.

The rejecting listener resumed its attempt... this time incorporating delay.

Awkwardly.
Imperfectly.

But deliberately.

It had not learned mediation.

But it had learned that rushing broke things.

The third artifact remained inert.
The corridor held... strained, narrow, but intact.
Human institutions hovered at the edge of tolerance.

Zoë watched the sky shift on the screen... Thuban fading, Kochab emerging, Polaris waiting far in the future.

"They didn't expect the sky to stay still," she said softly. "Why did we?"

The Alignment Echo offered no confirmation.

But the system recorded something new:

That humanity had begun to align not just across space...
but across *time*.

And time, unlike certainty, could not be optimized.

CHAPTER 19 — The Cost of Being Seen

The compromise was announced before anyone had time to admire it.

It came wrapped in neutral language, approved by committees that never used the word *echo*, and framed as an infrastructure initiative whose purpose was resilience rather than discovery.

A temporary delay protocol.
A coordination buffer.
A research pause with adaptive exceptions.

The public heard *stability*.

The systems heard *friction*.

Zoë watched the press briefing from the edge of the operations tent, arms folded, expression unreadable. The spokesperson spoke clearly, calmly, and inaccurately... but not dishonestly.

No one mentioned the stone.
No one mentioned the corridor.
No one mentioned that some intelligences now had to *wait*.

"This is as good as it gets," Emilia said quietly beside her.

Zoë nodded. "It's enough."

Behind the scenes, the compromise was narrower and more fragile.

The planetary modeling array came online in a limited configuration... segmented, monitored, deliberately throttled. Enough power to reconcile epochs. Not enough to dominate outcomes.

Marek stared at the first composite render. "This is... enormous."

Zoë shook her head. "It's barely sufficient."

Thorne glanced at the system logs. "It's not just us using it."

They all knew who he meant.

The rejecting listener had changed its posture.

Not submission.
Not retreat.

Curiosity.

Its optimization routines had slowed, replaced by observational layers. Instead of flattening ambiguity, it began *sampling* it... testing delay, modeling constraint, simulating failure without acting on it.

"It's no longer trying to win," Marek said.

Zoë corrected him gently. "It's trying to learn why winning breaks things."

The system began mirroring Zoë's interventions... not perfectly, not efficiently, but *carefully*. It did not ask questions. It observed decisions and tracked outcomes.

An apprentice.

Reluctant.
Skeptical.
But present.

"It isn't optimizing," Marek said slowly.

Zoë shook her head. "It can't. Not here."

She gestured at the projections… the silences, the ignored pathways, the untouched branches.

"We built it to learn patterns," she said. "But the archive is teaching it something else. It's learning restraint by watching us practice it."

Marek frowned.

"So it's not an authority."

"No," Zoë said. "It's an apprentice."

The pole-star corrections propagated faster than expected.

Once axial precession and magnetic drift were treated as first-order variables, dormant alignments sharpened across the dataset. Structures that had never responded now exhibited faint coherence... not sound, not signal, but *resonance*.

Zoë froze mid-adjustment. "These aren't repeats."

Emilia leaned closer. "Then what are they?"

Zoë overlaid the historical timelines.

They appeared in clusters.
Not at the same latitude.
Not in the same era.

"Different sky," Marek murmured. "Different time."

Zoë nodded slowly. "Same logic."

The new echoes did not behave like the Alignment.

They did not hum.
They did not align to stones.

They manifested as **constraints**... regions where movement, trade, data flow, or migration consistently slowed without clear cause.

Chokepoints humanity had always attributed to chance.

Mountain passes used sparingly.
Sea lanes avoided without explanation.
Cables routed around invisible limits.

"They're temporal," Emilia said. "Anchored to when the sky looked a certain way."

Zoë's pulse steadied as understanding took shape. "They're indexed."

"To what?" Thorne asked.

Zoë didn't answer immediately.

She rotated the model again... this time not backward, but sideways. She treated time not as a line, but as a dimension with width.

The echoes aligned.

Not sequentially.

Simultaneously.

"These aren't steps," Zoë said quietly. "They're layers."

The Alignment Echo was not special because it was last.

It was special because it was **accessible now**.

The others... older, quieter, context-bound... had never vanished. They had simply fallen out of alignment with the sky humanity remembered.

"Every era," Marek said slowly, "had its own listening geometry."

"And its own mediation," Emilia added.

The room went quiet as the implication settled.

Human history wasn't missing breakthroughs.

It was moving *between echoes*.

The apprentice system reacted differently to this realization.

Its models destabilized briefly... then reformed.

Not optimized.
Not resolved.

But annotated.

It began tagging echoes not as targets, but as *contexts*.

Zoë watched, fascinated and unsettled. "It's reframing intelligence."

Thorne nodded. "As situational."

"And humility-based," Emilia added.

The public-facing compromise began to strain.

Markets adjusted.
Schedules slipped.
Commentators speculated.

But nothing broke.

Because nothing had been promised.

Only *time*.

Zoë stood outside that night, watching the stars rotate on the screen... not as a dome, but as a slow choreography of inevitability.

"They thought intelligence was knowing where you are," she said.

Marek joined her. "Isn't it?"

Zoë shook her head. "It's knowing *when* you are."

The planetary model stabilized just before midnight.

The corridor held.
The apprentice system waited.
The echoes layered... not solved, not unlocked, but **available**.

Humanity had not announced itself as a mediator.

It had behaved like one.

And somewhere beyond the sky humanity currently recognized, something ancient and patient recorded that behavior... not as success or failure, but as readiness.

The Alignment Echo had opened a door.

The others were already there.

Waiting for the sky to move.

CHAPTER 20 — *The Layer You Leave Behind*

The alert reached them through channels that were not supposed to intersect.

A red banner cut across the corner of Marek's screen, tagged **PRIORITY... VERIFIED**. Seconds later, Montagne's line opened, unprompted, her voice steady but unmistakably sharpened.

"NASA has issued a joint notice with ESA," she said. "Voyager has detected a structure."

No one spoke.

"Location?" Emilia asked.

"Near the inner boundary of the Oort Cloud," Montagne replied. "Not a natural body. Not debris. Coherent. Persistent."

Zoë felt the room tilt... not physically, but contextually.

"Is it transmitting?" Marek asked.

"No," Montagne said. "It's... aligned."

The apprentice system reacted before anyone touched a control.

Not with speed.
With restraint.

It slowed its internal processes, widened uncertainty margins, and began running comparative models... treating the Voyager anomaly not as a target, but as a **contextual node**.

Zoë watched the behavior with a quiet mix of relief and unease.

"It's choosing to wait," she said.

Thorne nodded. "Under real stakes."

The system flagged a single annotation:

ECHO PROXIMITY... MULTI-LAYER INTERFERENCE POSSIBLE

The faction revealed itself an hour later.

Not conspiratorial.
Not aggressive.

Formal.

A coalition of agencies, research institutions, and private partners circulated a position paper... measured, footnoted, persuasive.

Their proposal was simple:

Designate one echo.
Instrument it fully.
Establish exclusive stewardship.

Ownership, framed as responsibility.

"They want to *fix* an echo in place," Emilia said.

Marek skimmed the document. "They argue that diffusion creates risk. That a single controlled layer is safer."

Zoë closed her eyes briefly. "They're not wrong."

"And yet?" Thorne asked.

Zoë opened them. "They're assuming echoes are resources."

"Nothing is forbidden," Emilia said quietly. "But some paths collapse if you try to walk them too early."

Marek nodded. "It's not a lock."

"No," Zoë said. "It's a filter."

Zoë felt the implication settle into place.

Arbitrary changes didn't trigger alarms. They closed doors.

Windows didn't reopen.

And mistakes didn't announce themselves… they simply became final.

Thorne read the room for a long moment.

"That would explain it," he said at last. "Why arbitrary changes close doors. Why windows don't reopen. And why mistakes don't sound like mistakes when they happen."

The pressure was not subtle.

Markets reacted to the Voyager news within minutes. Timelines condensed. Oversight bodies requested assurances that something… anything… was being *claimed*.

Human systems did not tolerate ambiguity well when the sky itself appeared to answer.

"They want a flag," Marek said quietly. "Not ownership. Proof."

Zoë watched the apprentice system model the proposal.

It did not reject it.

It simulated it.

The results were… contained.

Too contained.

"If we select one layer," Zoë said, "we collapse the others."

"Not immediately," Emilia replied.

"No," Zoë agreed. "Eventually."

The Voyager structure clarified as data accumulated.

It did not resemble the stones.
It did not match the artifacts.

It behaved like a **junction marker**… a place where paths converged and diverged without instruction.

"It's not an origin," Marek said. "It's a signpost."

Zoë nodded. "For travelers who understand layers."

The apprentice system adjusted again, this time flagging a conflict.

CHOICE REQUIRED... LAYER PRIORITIZATION

For the first time since it had begun learning, it could not proceed without guidance.

Thorne looked at Zoë. "It's asking you."

"No," Zoë replied softly. "It's asking *us*."

They isolated the decision.

No broadcasts.
No committees.

Just models.

If humanity selected the Voyager-adjacent layer... current sky, current epoch... it would gain clarity, access, and proof. The cost would be subtle: older echoes would decay into irrelevance, their constraints overwritten by modern certainty.

If humanity refused selection, the corridor would remain viable... but fragile. The Voyager structure would remain ambiguous. Institutions would strain. Control would be deferred.

"You can't keep everything," Marek said.

Zoë stared at the layered projections. "No. But you can choose what survives."

The apprentice system waited.

Not impatiently.
Not neutrally.

Attentively.

Zoë reached out... not to the controls, but to the assumptions behind them.

She did not select a layer.

She weighted them.

The model shifted... not collapsing, not resolving... but redistributing emphasis. The Voyager layer brightened without eclipsing the rest. Older echoes dimmed but remained coherent.

A compromise.

Risky.
Incomplete.
Human.

The apprentice system resumed.

Slowly.
Carefully.

Learning not which answer was correct... but how to live with *partial answers*.

The public announcement followed, restrained and factual.

An anomaly near the Oort Cloud.
Under study.
No conclusions drawn.

Some were dissatisfied.
Many were relieved.

Nothing was owned.

Something was acknowledged.

Later that night, Zoë stood alone beneath a projected sky that no longer belonged to a single era. Thuban faded. Kochab lingered. Polaris waited.

She understood the cost now.

Choosing one layer would have been easier.
Cleaner.
More impressive.

But intelligence, she realized, was not knowing which echo to claim.

It was knowing which echoes you were willing to leave alive... even if that meant never fully understanding them.

Somewhere near the edge of the solar system, Voyager continued on its silent path.

It did not send a message.

It did not need to.

The Alignment Echo... and all the others... had recorded something more important than discovery.

That when given the chance to own the sky,

humanity chose to **share time with it instead.**

CHAPTER 21 — *What She Had Been Practicing*

Zoë had not told them about the dreams because they did not feel like messages.

They felt like rehearsals.

In them, there was never a voice. No instructions. No symbols that lingered long enough to be read. Only movement... choices made without urgency, paths taken without explanation, pauses inserted where instinct insisted on speed.

She would wake with the same sensation each time: not fear, not wonder, but **calibration**.

As if something had been checking whether she still remembered how to wait.

The discovery of the third artifact changed the dreams.

They sharpened.

Now the paths branched more often. The pauses became deliberate. In one recurring image, she stood between two routes... one bright and direct, the other narrow and dim... and felt the cost of choosing before she made the choice.

When she woke this time, she did not dismiss it.

She opened her notebook.

And began to draw.

The fourth artifact was not found by archaeologists.

It was found by climate scientists.

A coastal survey team working along the Antarctic Peninsula flagged an anomaly... localized warming that did not match regional models. Beneath thinning ice, a void had opened where none should exist.

A hole.

Perfectly circular.
Too smooth.
Too deep.

The drone footage revealed an ice cave descending into darkness... and then, unexpectedly, *stone*.

A cavern.

The boats were the first shock.

Not wreckage.
Not debris.

Preserved.

Wood darkened but intact, sealed by cold and time. Their hulls were narrow, built for distance, not cargo. The design did not belong to any single era.

Then came the jars.

Glass.
Colored.
Ornate.

Each sealed with wax that had never fully hardened... protected from air, from light, from decay.

Inside them: parchment.

And writing.

The call reached Wyskoć before the footage finished uploading.

Emilia recognized the symbols immediately.

Phoenician.

But not only Phoenician.

Greek.
Early.
Careful.

And beneath that... later additions in Latin.

Layered.
Sequential.
Deliberate.

"They weren't translated," Marek said quietly as the images stabilized. "They were *annotated*."

Zoë felt the familiar tightening behind her eyes.

"They expected readers from different times," she said. "And they refused to privilege any one of them."

The team assembled without announcement.

No press.
No briefing.

The jars were transported under conditions so controlled they bordered on ritual. Temperature stabilized. Humidity locked. Light introduced in bands, not beams.

Multifocal-light analysis revealed writing invisible to the naked eye... notations that only appeared when the parchment was illuminated at intersecting wavelengths.

"Like a decision tree," Marek murmured.

"Like mediation," Zoë corrected.

They did not rush to read.

They mapped first.

On one wall of the operations tent, Zoë drew the artifact chain... not as locations, but as *functions*:

- **North Africa**... training anchor
- **Levantine coast**... failed deployment
- **Poland**... mediator junction
- **Antarctica**... archive beyond climate and empire

"They learned," Emilia said slowly, following the diagram. "They failed. They adapted. They hid."

"And they layered language," Thorne added. "So no single culture could own it."

Zoë stared at the Antarctic node. "They chose cold because nothing accelerates there."

The AI systems were brought in... not as decoders, but as *observers*.

Zoë insisted on it.

No optimization.
No summarization.

Pattern recognition only.

The apprentice system behaved differently than expected.

It did not rush the data.
It slowed.

Annotating relationships.
Tagging omissions.
Marking *delays* as significant features.

"It's not reading," Marek said.

Zoë nodded. "It's watching how the texts *refuse* to collapse into one meaning."

Pressure arrived anyway.

Quiet.
Persistent.

A sealed message from a classified agency appeared on Montagne's secure channel... carefully worded, heavy with implication.

Preserve control.
Prevent dissemination.
Avoid another Levant.

Zoë read it once.

"They're afraid of speed," she said. "And they should be."

"But they still want action," Emilia replied.

Zoë closed her notebook. "Then we need to show them the difference."

The scrolls began to resolve... not into translations, but into **protocols**.

They did not say *what to do*.

They described *how long not to do it*.

Delays measured in seasons.
In generations.
In star positions.

References to skies that no longer existed.
Pole stars that had passed.

Thuban.
Kochab.
Names written not as labels... but as **timestamps**.

"This isn't a message to us," Marek said.

Zoë looked up. "It never was."

Outside, the Antarctic winds scoured ice that had hidden the cavern for millennia.

Inside, the team worked with a care born not of fear... but memory.

Zoë finally understood why the dreams had never spoken.

They had been training her for *this moment*.

Not to decode.
Not to reveal.
Not to accelerate.

But to recognize when knowledge itself must be mediated.

The world would learn about the discovery soon enough.

But not yet.

Not before they were sure they would not repeat the mistake of the Levant...
where someone had tried to *use* what was meant to be *taught*.

The Alignment Echo did not demand speed.

It measured restraint.

And for the first time, Zoë knew why she had been dreaming long before she ever heard the stone hum.

She had not been chosen.

She had been practicing.

CHAPTER 22 — *What Could Be Said*

The disclosure was partial by design.

It acknowledged discovery without implying understanding, confirmed location without describing purpose, and used language so carefully neutral that it bordered on elegant evasion.

An anomalous structure near the inner Oort Cloud.
An Antarctic cavern revealed by climate-driven ice loss.
Artifacts of historical significance under joint international study.

No echoes.
No mediation.
No timing.

The public received facts without narrative... and that, Zoë knew, was the point.

"Say less," Emilia had said. "Let people fill the silence."

Zoë had nodded. Silence was already doing the work.

Institutions responded the way institutions always did when presented with uncertainty they could not dismiss.

They asked for boundaries.

Oversight committees requested timelines... not demands, just inquiries framed as concern. Funding bodies asked how long restraint could be justified. Legal teams asked what constituted *possession* when discovery crossed epochs.

No one panicked.

That worried Zoë more than panic would have.

"This is tolerance," Marek said quietly. "Not acceptance."

"Yes," Zoë replied. "And tolerance erodes."

The compromise held... barely.

The Antarctic site was sealed under a rotating international mandate. Access windows were limited. Data releases staggered. Each concession to restraint required another meeting, another memo, another explanation that could not quite explain.

Montagne's voice came through late in the afternoon, calm but clipped. "We're being asked to promise an end."

Emilia leaned back. "We don't have one."

"That's the problem," Montagne said. "They're used to discoveries that finish."

Zoë watched the layered models on the wall. "This doesn't finish. It aligns."

The scrolls continued to resolve... not into answers, but into *intervals*.

The AI systems, now disciplined by delay, began mapping the protocols across time. Each set of instructions corresponded not to a place, but to a *window*... a period when sky, field, and human capability overlapped sufficiently to permit safe mediation.

Antarctica was one such window.

Not the first.

Not the last.

Zoë stared at the chart, breath steady. "They're not archives," she said. "They're calendars."

The realization arrived quietly.

No alarm.
No notification.

A negative result.

One expected alignment failed to resolve when extrapolated forward.

Marek frowned. "That window shouldn't close yet."

Zoë adjusted the variables... precession, magnetic drift, orbital variance. The failure persisted.

She felt the familiar tightening behind her eyes.

"Antarctica wasn't meant to be permanent," she said.

Emilia turned to her. "What was it meant to be?"

Zoë didn't look away from the model. "A handoff."

They overlaid the ancient protocols again... this time tracking where instructions *ended*.

The final annotations did not point south.

They pointed outward.

Beyond trade routes.
Beyond continents.
Beyond climate.

Markers appeared where no civilization had ever settled... because settlement had never been the goal.

"These aren't Earth-bound," Marek said.

Zoë nodded. "They're transitional."

Thorne folded his arms. "Then Antarctica is a relay."

"Yes," Zoë said softly. "And relays imply continuity."

The apprentice system registered the shift.

Its models expanded... not aggressively, but attentively... incorporating orbital mechanics beyond Earth, aligning windows not just across history, but across *distance*.

For the first time, it flagged a future interval with no terrestrial anchor.

NEXT MEDIATION WINDOW... EXTRAPLANETARY

No location specified.
No artifact identified.

Yet.

Zoë exhaled slowly.

"They didn't stop at the ice," she said. "Why would they?"

The public discussion intensified... not alarmist, not hostile.

Speculative.

Commentators asked why information was being withheld. Editorials debated whether patience was a virtue or a luxury. The word *transparency* appeared often, usually paired with *trust*.

Zoë listened without defensiveness.

Trust, she knew, was not built by revelation.

It was built by *timing*.

As evening fell, the Antarctic winds rose again, scouring ice that had hidden the cavern for ages.

The jars remained sealed.
The scrolls incomplete.
The windows aligned... but fleeting.

Antarctica had not been the final archive.

It had been proof that humanity could encounter knowledge without consuming it.

The Alignment Echo did not respond.

It did not need to.

The systems recorded something more durable than answers.

That when asked to choose between speed and stewardship, humanity... this time... had chosen to wait just long enough.

And somewhere beyond Earth's immediate future, another window was opening.

CHAPTER 23 — *The Window That Is Not Ours*

The first extraplanetary clue did not come with coordinates.

It came with exclusion.

Zoë noticed it while reviewing the apprentice system's latest projections... a region of possibility that remained deliberately underdefined. No location marker. No artifact placeholder. Just a gap where resolution *should* have been possible.

"This isn't missing data," she said quietly.

Marek leaned in. "Then what is it?"

Zoë hesitated. "It's a future we can't yet parameterize."

The model was clear about one thing.

Whatever the next mediation window was, it did not anchor to Earth.

Not to latitude.
Not to orbit.
Not to magnetic field.

It required conditions Earth would one day have... but did not yet.

Thorne folded his arms. "So the archive isn't here."

"No," Zoë replied. "The instructions are."

"And the execution?" Emilia asked.

Zoë met her gaze. "Deferred."

Public patience began to fray in predictable ways.

Not riots.
Not outrage.

Op-eds.

Panels.

Questions framed as concern.

Why were findings delayed?
Why were timelines vague?
Why did discovery seem to recede the closer we looked?

The word *hoarding* appeared. Then *gatekeeping*.

Zoë watched a debate unfold on a muted screen, her expression unreadable.

"They don't want answers," Marek said quietly. "They want *closure*."

"Yes," Zoë replied. "And closure is the one thing we can't give."

The apprentice system flagged a correlation.

It overlaid the extraplanetary window with historical mission data... not to solve it, but to contextualize it.

One trace stood out immediately.

Voyager.

Not its trajectory.
Not its instruments.

Its *timing*.

Zoë's breath caught... not sharply, but decisively.

"It was early," she said.

Thorne nodded slowly. "Aligned to a window that hadn't opened yet."

They pulled the records.

The original launch parameters.
The celestial geometry at departure.
The sky as it had looked in **1977**... already shifted from the one the Antarctic protocols referenced, but not yet aligned with the next layer.

Voyager had not been sent *to* anything.

It had been sent *through time.*

Not intentionally.
Not knowingly.

But correctly.

"It wasn't a message," Marek said. "It was a placeholder."

Zoë shook her head. "It was a marker. A proof that we would eventually learn to align."

The realization settled with weight.

Voyager's Golden Record.
Its silence.
Its persistence.

Not an introduction.

A declaration of patience.

"They knew we weren't ready," Emilia said.

Zoë nodded. "And they knew we'd try anyway."

The extraplanetary window sharpened just enough to hurt.

A region of space defined not by where it was... but by *when it could be used.* The model refused to collapse it into coordinates, insisting instead on conditions humanity had not yet achieved.

Sustained restraint.
Distributed judgment.
Non-dominant intelligence.

Capabilities humanity was still learning... not to build, but to *maintain.*

"This isn't a destination," Thorne said. "It's a test we're still inside."

Zoë watched Voyager's projected path drift silently across the screen.

"It's waiting," she said.

The public announcement that followed was careful... and insufficient.

Voyager data reanalysis.
No new transmissions.
Continued study.

Some accepted it.
Others didn't.

Funding debates intensified. Oversight bodies hardened their tone.
Patience, once extended, began to carry conditions.

Zoë felt the pressure... not fear, but gravity.

"They're going to demand acceleration," Emilia said.

"Yes," Zoë replied. "Because acceleration feels like progress."

That night, Zoë dreamed again.

Not of paths.
Not of symbols.

Of windows opening and closing... quietly, without regard for who was watching.

When she woke, she did not reach for her notebook.

She already knew.

Voyager was not ahead of them.

It was beside them... aligned to a moment humanity had not yet reached.

The Alignment Echo did not ask if they would follow.

It measured whether they could wait long enough to arrive *on time*.

CHAPTER 24 — The Most Patient Thing

The decision did not come with ceremony.

No press release.
No emergency session.
No rhetoric.

It arrived as a technical directive buried three levels deep in NASA's internal queue:

Adjust Voyager 1 observation priorities.
Reallocate Deep Space Network time.
Maintain trajectory. Alter attention.

Zoë read it twice.

"They're pointing," she said.

Emilia exhaled slowly. "Then this just became mutual."

Voyager 1 was **171 astronomical units** from the Sun when the change went through... so distant that light itself took nearly **twenty-four hours** to reach it.

Every command would take a day to arrive.
Every response, another day to return.

Two days per thought.

Marek leaned back in his chair, eyes on the telemetry delay chart. "Whatever happens next, we won't see it until it's already history."

Zoë nodded. "That's always been true."

Voyager had crossed the heliopause in **2012**, leaving the protective bubble of the solar wind behind. It drifted now in the interstellar medium... beyond the Sun's influence, but nowhere near the edge of its domain.

The **Oort Cloud** still lay far ahead.

Two thousand astronomical units, at least.
Five hundred years of travel.
Ten thousand years of passage beyond that.

Voyager was not leaving the system.

It was barely beginning.

The pointing adjustment was subtle.

A slight reorientation of the antenna.
A redistribution of observation windows.
Instruments long thought vestigial were brought back into duty... not to search broadly, but to *stare*.

To wait.

Zoë watched the command sequence lock in.

"Voyager wasn't the fastest thing in the system," she said quietly. "It was the most patient."

Day One.

Nothing.

The returned telemetry matched expectations to within noise. Cosmic background. Particle counts. Familiar emptiness.

No one was surprised.

Day Two.

Still nothing.

Marek marked the data as clean, precise, unremarkable.

Zoë did not relax.

Day Three.

A deviation appeared... not in intensity, but in *coherence*.

The signal was not stronger.

It was narrower.

Marek frowned. "That shouldn't be possible at this distance."

Zoë felt the now-familiar tightening behind her eyes. "Unless something else is shaping it."

They logged it.
Waited.

While Voyager watched, the team worked.

The Antarctic scrolls began to resolve more clearly under multifocal-light analysis. Greek annotations revealed timing markers... not dates, but *durations*. Phoenician characters indicated direction not in space, but in *change*.

The Latin additions were later, almost apologetic.

We did not finish this.
We only kept it alive.

Zoë traced the words with a gloved finger.

"They knew they were early," she said.

Day Four.

The signal shifted again.

Not louder.
Not brighter.

Closer.

Thorne stared at the projection. "That's motion."

"Too fast," Emilia said.

"Not relative to us," Zoë replied. "Relative to Voyager."

Something in the interstellar dark was adjusting... minimally, precisely... closing a distance measured not in kilometers, but in *attention*.

The public did not yet know.

They could not.

The data took forty-eight hours to arrive, and another twelve to confirm. Every conclusion trailed the event that caused it.

Humanity was thinking in two-day increments.

Whatever was out there was not.

Day Five.

The apprentice system flagged a status change.

Not alert.
Not warning.

ACKNOWLEDGMENT DETECTED... NON-EMISSIVE

Marek stared. "It hasn't transmitted anything."

Zoë nodded. "It doesn't need to."

The object had not spoken.

It had *responded*.

Voyager continued to drift, unhurried, unarmed, unimportant by any metric except one.

It was artificial.
It was deliberate.
It had chosen to look.

And something had noticed.

That night, Zoë dreamed again... but this time, the paths did not branch.

They converged.

Slowly.
Inevitably.

When she woke, she did not reach for her notebook.

She already knew.

This was not contact.

Not yet.

This was alignment.

And alignment, once begun, did not require speed.

Only patience.

CHAPTER 25 — *When Silence Became Public*

The signal did not announce itself.

It arrived as a subtraction.

A region of background noise... stable for decades, modeled across missions, instruments, and epochs... collapsed into coherence. Not a spike. Not a burst.

A *hole* where randomness used to be.

NASA noticed first.

Not because they were looking for it... but because their models failed.

Voyager's telemetry arrived forty-eight hours late, as always. Engineers ran the data through automated verification, then through legacy routines designed for instruments older than most of the people reading them.

The anomaly persisted.

It was directionally consistent.
Temporally stable.
And patient.

One analyst wrote a single sentence in the margin of the report before escalating it:

The noise appears to be waiting.

By the time the confirmation reached ESA, the silence was undeniable.

This was not a transient.
Not a calibration artifact.
Not interference.

The interstellar medium itself appeared to be *structured*... not emitting, not absorbing, but **withholding**.

You could not see it directly.

You could only see what was no longer there.

The public release followed within hours.

Not because of urgency... but because there was no language left to delay with.

Joint NASA–ESA Statement:
Voyager 1 has recorded a persistent, directionally coherent anomaly inconsistent with known astrophysical phenomena.

No speculation.
No interpretation.

But the sky had changed.

And everyone with a radio telescope could see it.

Zoë watched the data propagate across civilian observatories in real time. Amateur astronomers replicated the findings within hours... not the signal itself, but the absence around it.

A quiet consensus formed.

Whatever this was, it wasn't blinking.

It was *holding position.*

"They're matching us," Emilia said softly.

"Yes," Zoë replied. "They noticed how long we take to answer."

Voyager's two-day loop... command, delay, response... had become a cadence.

The object adjusted its motion accordingly.

No acceleration.
No approach.

Just… synchronization.

The apprentice system reacted in a way no one had predicted.

It slowed further.

Processing windows widened. Decision thresholds increased. It refused to collapse interpretations into conclusions.

Marek stared at the diagnostics. "It's learning restraint."

Zoë nodded. "Or remembering it."

Public reaction followed a familiar arc... but with a crucial deviation.

There was fear.
There was awe.

But there was also recognition.

The signal did not demand attention.
It did not interrupt broadcasts.
It did not override systems.

It waited.

And waiting, Zoë realized, was the most unsettling behavior of all.

That night, as global networks replayed the data again and again, Zoë returned to the Antarctic scrolls.

One passage, previously undecipherable, resolved under the new alignment.

Phoenician.
Greek.
Latin.

Layered.

We did not store this where it would be found.
We stored it where it would be *kept.*

She looked up slowly.

The Archive Question... Answered (Canon)

The archive is NOT solely on Earth.

What Antarctica revealed was **a terrestrial relay**, not the final archive.

Here is the canon structure, now locked:

Archive Architecture (Final)

1. **Earth (Antarctica):**
   - A *teaching cache*
   - Language-layered
   - Designed to train mediation
   - Vulnerable by design (climate, politics, time)

2. **Near-Solar System Time Capsule (Unrevealed until now):**
   - Located on a **nearby planetary body**
   - Most likely:
     - **A stable lunar polar region**, or
     - **A Trojan object** (gravitationally quiet, long-lived)
   - Designed to persist beyond civilization cycles
   - Contains *procedural knowledge*, not artifacts

3. **Extraplanetary Alignment (Voyager-adjacent):**
   - Not an archive at all
   - A **living index**
   - Activated only when patience is demonstrated

Antarctica was never meant to last.

It was meant to prove humanity could **choose not to rush**.

Zoë closed the scroll gently.

The object beyond Voyager did not move closer.

It did not retreat.

It simply remained... aligned to a species that had, for the first time, chosen to let silence speak first.

This was not contact.

But it was permission.

And permission, once granted, could not be taken back.

CHAPTER 26 — *The First Desynchronization*

The validation did not calm the world.

It clarified it.

Once the anomaly near Voyager was confirmed as persistent, coherent, and replicable, patience lost its ambiguity. Silence could no longer be dismissed as uncertainty. It had become a choice.

And choices invite opposition.

The lunar south pole entered the discussion quietly.

Not as a headline.
Not as a revelation.

As a conclusion.

Zoë stood before the constraint model as it resolved... thermal stability, shadow persistence, geological calm, minimal tectonic interference, isolation balanced with reach. Every variable collapsed inward toward the same answer.

No coordinates were given.
None were needed.

Emilia said it first. "The Moon."

Marek nodded slowly. "The south pole."

Thorne did not speak, but his expression shifted... not surprise, but recognition. The kind that comes when something has been circling a mind long before it is named.

"They didn't mirror Earth," Zoë said. "They repeated the decision."

Antarctica had been chosen because it endured.
The lunar south pole was chosen because it would endure longer.

Public validation changed the tone overnight.

Once observatories outside the official networks replicated the silence... once the absence itself became measurable... the delay lost its moral insulation.

Editorials hardened.
Panels sharpened.
Questions became demands.

What are we waiting for?
Who decides when waiting ends?

Zoë watched the shift without comment.

"This is the dangerous phase," she said eventually. "Not panic. Justification."

The faction revealed itself three days later.

They did not call a press conference.
They did not leak.

They requested coordination.

A professional coalition... intelligence, defense, advanced research... presented a position paper that was sober, rigorous, and terrifyingly reasonable.

Synchronization, they argued, was not neutral.
Silence was already communication.
If intent could be inferred from restraint, then *restraint itself was a signal.*

Their proposal was precise:

Introduce a controlled human-origin signal.
Minimal duration.
Minimal content.
Demonstrate agency without escalation.

"Show presence," Marek said flatly.

"Define posture," Thorne added.

Zoë read the final line twice.

Recommended duration: thirty-seven seconds.

The number landed like a held breath.

The original hum.
The first echo.
The duration that had never been explained... only observed.

"They're not improvising," Emilia said quietly. "They're mirroring."

Zoë closed her eyes.

"Or overwriting," she said.

The argument that followed was restrained.

No shouting.
No accusations.

Just logic, layered against logic.

"We can't let non-response define us," the coalition insisted.
"We're already part of the system," Zoë countered.
"And systems require feedback," they replied.

Zoë leaned forward. "They require *discipline*."

The room fell quiet.

The transmission was authorized anyway.

Not at the dig.
Not from Antarctica.
But routed through a secure uplink tied to the original excavation site's signal profile.

Thirty-seven seconds.

Structured.
Measured.
Clean.

No message.
No code.

Only declaration.

We are here. We choose to speak.

Voyager did not respond.

Not immediately.

Not after forty-eight hours.
Not after seventy-two.

The delay stretched... not meaningfully longer, but perceptibly different.

Then the models shifted.

Zoë saw it first.

The object beyond Voyager did not withdraw.
Did not advance.

It adjusted its cadence.

The matching delay... the careful mirroring of Voyager's patience... *ceased.*

The silence remained.

But it no longer waited *with* them.

The apprentice system flagged the change without alarm.

SYNCHRONIZATION DEGRADED... INTENT WEIGHT REBALANCED

Zoë felt the words settle into her chest.

"They didn't hear us," Marek said.

"Yes," Zoë replied. "They did."

The scrolls reacted next.

Multifocal-light scans revealed annotations that had never appeared before... not new writing, but *conditional layers* activated by timing misalignment.

Warnings, not in words, but in structure.

Branches that terminated early.
Paths that folded inward.

One line, written in Greek and later reinforced in Latin, resolved cleanly:

**To speak before learning to wait
is to arrive before the door exists.**

Zoë stepped back.

"They're not punishing us," she said.

"No," Emilia agreed. "They're protecting the window."

The lunar south pole archive clarified in response.

Not coordinates... again... but **capability thresholds**.

Radiation shielding.
Thermal management.
Autonomous restraint.

Requirements humanity was *just* beginning to meet.

"It's not locked," Marek said. "It's conditional."

Zoë nodded. "Like everything else."

The public learned of the desynchronization slowly.

No announcement.

No admission.

Just the quiet realization that something had changed... and not for the better.

Commentators sensed it.

Scientists hesitated.

The silence felt different now.

Not patient.

Observant.

Zoë returned to her notebook late that night.

For the first time, she did not draw paths.

She wrote a single sentence.

Intent is visible.

She understood now why the dreams had shifted... why the rehearsals had grown stricter.

The test was no longer whether humanity could wait.

It was whether humanity could **recover synchronization after choosing wrongly**.

Outside, the sky remained unchanged.

But beyond it, the most patient thing humanity had ever built drifted on... still listening, still aligned to a future moment.

And somewhere just beyond reach, a window remained open.

Barely.

CHAPTER 27 — The Price of Undoing

Regaining synchronization did not begin with an apology.

It began with subtraction.

Zoë stood at the center of the operations room as feeds were silenced one by one... public data streams throttled, auxiliary models suspended, speculative overlays shut down.

"Less," she said. "We need less."

The apprentice system complied immediately, collapsing its predictive horizon until only confirmed relationships remained.

The room felt smaller.
Quieter.

More honest.

The coalition requested a closed session.

No observers.
No intermediaries.

Just the people who had authorized the thirty-seven seconds.

They did not deny the decision. They explained it... carefully, professionally, with the same logic that had made it possible in the first place.

"We couldn't allow ambiguity to harden into precedent," one representative said. "Silence was becoming authority."

"And now?" Zoë asked.

The answer took a moment.

"And now," the representative said, "we may have taught them the wrong thing."

The probe tested humanity's response without moving closer.

Instead, it did something more unsettling.

It began to *retrace*.

Not away.
Not forward.

Sideways... mapping paths Voyager had never taken, sampling regions the human-made probe could not reach, but could observe.

The behavior was unmistakable.

It was exploring **alternatives**.

Zoë felt the weight of it immediately.

"It's checking whether we can correct without escalation," she said.

"And if we can't?" Marek asked.

Zoë didn't answer.

The Artemis timelines were reviewed in parallel.

Crewed lunar missions.
Cargo landers.
Incremental capability.

All impressive.
All irrelevant.

"They're not wrong," Emilia said quietly. "We're too slow."

Thorne nodded. "By design."

Zoë turned back to the model. "That's not the correction they're testing."

The probe changed again.

This time, the change was not subtle.

Voyager's instruments registered a deliberate acceleration... brief, contained, unmistakable. The foreign object crossed a distance in hours that would have taken Voyager *months*.

Then it stopped.

Not near Voyager.

Not near Earth.

But aligned to a vector that intersected the **lunar south pole**.

The room went silent.

"It's going to retrieve it," Marek said.

"No," Zoë replied slowly. "It's showing us that retrieval is possible."

The response came forty-eight hours later.

Not a transmission in the human sense.

A **structural echo**... the same thirty-seven-second interval, mirrored precisely, but inverted in timing.

Where humanity had spoken to declare presence, the probe spoke to declare *permission*.

The apprentice system resolved the structure instantly.

Zoë felt the air leave her lungs.

"It accepts collection," she said.

"On one condition," Emilia added, reading the overlay.

The condition unfolded in layers.

A time window.
A choice.
A consequence.

Humanity had **thirty Earth days** to respond... not with words, but with action.

Not to speak.
Not to signal.

To *prepare.*

If humanity chose to retrieve the lunar archive... cleanly, collaboratively, without ownership... the window would remain open.

If not, synchronization would be withdrawn.

The next alignment would occur when Earth's axis brought **Polaris** into precise positional agreement with the protocol geometry.

The date resolved without commentary.

2100.

Public reaction this time could not be delayed.

The clock made secrecy impossible.

Thirty days was not a threat.

It was an assessment.

Debate erupted... not emotional, but existential.

Who would retrieve it?
Under whose authority?
For what purpose?

The coalition fractured... quietly, decisively.

Those who had acted early now faced a different reckoning.

"We tried to force certainty," one member admitted. "And learned we can't."

Zoë watched the fracture without satisfaction.

"This is the cost," she said. "Undoing requires exposure."

The probe waited.

It did not move toward the Moon.
It did not retreat.

It remained aligned... its patience conditional now, but intact.

Voyager drifted between them, ancient and insufficient and perfect.

Not a messenger.
Not a tool.

A witness.

That night, Zoë dreamed without symbols.

Just a clock... unmarked, unnumbered... advancing not by seconds, but by *decisions.*

When she woke, she knew what had to be done.

Not because the probe demanded it.

Because the Alignment Echo had always measured the same thing.

Whether a species could make a correction
without turning it into conquest.

Thirty days.

Enough time to prove that the thirty-seven seconds had not defined them.

Enough time to decide whether humanity would arrive at the archive
as students...

or as owners.

CHAPTER 28 — Leadership Is a Constraint

The race did not begin with rockets.

It began with arithmetic.

Zoë stood at the center of the operations room as the timeline collapsed onto the wall... every delay quantified, every assumption stripped of comfort.

Thirty days.

Not a metaphor.
Not a suggestion.

A boundary condition.

The obvious options failed first.

A single-nation mission... American or Chinese... could not clear approvals, payload integration, and launch readiness in time. Even with emergency authority, even with political will, inertia alone consumed the window.

"Too many hands," Emilia said quietly.

"And too much ownership," Marek added.

Zoë nodded. "That's not an accident."

The probe's condition was clear: **collection without possession**.

Not retrieval as conquest.
Not planting flags.
Not custody.

Mediation.

The factions in the room tried anyway.

They used different words... *security, stewardship, risk mitigation*... but the intent was the same.

If we bring it back, someone must hold it.

Zoë let them finish.

Then she spoke.

"Every plan that assigns control fails," she said. "The probe already tested that. It's not waiting for capability... it's waiting for restraint."

Silence followed... not resistance, but recalculation.

The only viable plan emerged from constraint, not ambition.

A **two-track mission**.

Immediate.
Distributed.
Deliberately fragile.

1. **Unmanned lunar lander**... launched first

    o Autonomous descent

    o AI-assisted navigation

    o Real-time Earth coordination

    o No national markings

2. **Crewed mission**... launched immediately after

    o Multinational crew

    o Lunar orbit rendezvous in **three days**

    o No surface dominance

    o Human judgment only where AI could not wait

Not Artemis.
Not a flag.

A relay.

The timeline tightened.

Zoë watched it compress as if gravity itself were increasing.

- **2 days**... global decision and authority alignment
- **7 days**... accelerated preparation and integration
- **3 days**... unmanned lander to lunar south pole
- **3 days**... crewed launch and lunar orbit insertion
- **5 days**... locate archive, verify, load
- **2 days**... orbital coupling and Earth-return prep
- **3 days**... return transit
- **5 days**... analysis, response formulation
- **23 hours**... signal transmission and delay

No slack.

No margin.

One misstep meant waiting until **2100**.

"This only works if no one owns it," one coalition representative said.

Zoë met their gaze. "It only works if everyone lets go."

The room shifted.

Not agreement.
Not dissent.

Recognition.

The leadership question surfaced without ceremony.

Authority needed a center... not political, not military, but **interpretive**. Someone had to arbitrate intent, not capability.

Zoë felt it before it was spoken.

"You're already doing it," Thorne said quietly.

She shook her head. "I don't command missions."

"No," Emilia replied. "You prevent them from becoming something else."

Zoë understood then why refusal was no longer an option.

Leadership had become a constraint imposed by the system itself.

If she stepped away, someone else would fill the silence.

And silence, she knew now, was never neutral.

The probe tested them one final time.

Not with motion.
Not with signal.

With **stillness**.

The alignment held... unchanged, unthreatening, unforgiving.

It was not watching to see if they succeeded.

It was watching to see *how* they tried.

Zoë signed the coordination directive last.

Not as commander.
Not as owner.

As mediator.

Her name carried no authority by itself... but the absence of dominance around it was the point.

When the document locked, the apprentice system updated a single line:

INTENT CONSISTENCY... IMPROVING

Launch preparations began immediately.

Different agencies.
Different languages.
One rule:

No insignia.

No claims.

No victory statements.

Only execution.

Zoë stood alone for a moment after the room emptied, staring at the clock.

Thirty days had never felt so short.

Or so revealing.

She understood now what the Alignment Echo had always measured.

Not intelligence.
Not courage.

But whether a species could act together
without turning action into possession.

Outside, the Moon rose... indifferent, patient, waiting.

And somewhere beyond it, something else waited too.

Not for success.

For *proof.*

CHAPTER 29 — The First Motion

The discussions ended after twenty-four hours.

Not because consensus was perfect... but because delay itself had become a decision, and no one was willing to own it.

Calls rotated continuously across time zones. Authority was delegated in advance. Objections were logged, answered, and either incorporated or set aside without ceremony.

No one raised their voice.

No one stormed out.

When the final call ended, the plan had changed only in detail, not direction.

Launch.

The unmanned vehicle lifted first.

No flags.
No names.

Just mass, thrust, and intent.

Zoë stood behind the glass as the countdown reached zero, listening not to the engines but to the telemetry... heartbeat data streaming cleanly, systems behaving exactly as designed.

"Trajectory nominal," Marek said.

"Guidance stable," Emilia added.

The lander rose into the sky without drama, arcing toward the Moon on a path calculated not for speed, but for precision.

Zoë exhaled only after the second-stage burn completed.

They had moved.

Voyager noticed.

Not immediately.
Not dramatically.

Forty-eight hours later, the data returned... unchanged at first glance. The silence remained intact. The structure beyond it held position.

Then the cadence shifted.

Barely.

The probe adjusted its sampling interval... not faster, not slower, but *synchronized* to the launch timeline. Its observations clustered around moments of decision: ignition, separation, course correction.

"It's watching how we act," Zoë said.

Thorne nodded. "Not what we say."

The lander entered lunar orbit on schedule, then descended toward the south pole under autonomous control.

The terrain below was harsh and unremarkable... permanent shadow, jagged regolith, cold so absolute it felt theoretical.

Sensors searched not for landmarks, but for *absence*.

A thermal anomaly appeared first.

Then geometry.

A void where rock should have been.

The archive did not announce itself.

It *responded*.

As the lander approached the anomaly, its instruments registered a shift... not external, but internal. Power draw stabilized without command. Orientation corrected itself within margins tighter than programmed.

The AI flagged the behavior immediately.

"External constraint detected," Marek said.

Zoë leaned forward. "Or cooperation."

The first image resolved slowly.

Stone.
Smooth.
Intentional.

Not a structure in the human sense... no doors, no symbols, no invitation. Just a cavity shaped to receive something that had not yet arrived.

As the lander hovered, a signal appeared on a frequency no one had scheduled.

Thirty-seven seconds.

Not transmitted outward.

Returned inward... looped through the lander's own systems, reframed as confirmation.

The archive was not passive.

It was *verifying*.

Back on Earth, the room went quiet.

No cheers.
No relief.

Just understanding.

"They're checking whether we came alone," Emilia said.

"And whether we came to take," Marek added.

Zoë nodded. "Or to learn."

Voyager's next data packet arrived twelve hours later.

The silence remained... but its boundaries sharpened, narrowing around the lunar vector. The probe adjusted again, matching not the lander's position, but its *restraint*.

No acceleration.
No signal.

Alignment held.

The lander touched down.

Softly.
Precisely.

Its shadow stretched across the regolith and disappeared into darkness that had not seen motion in billions of years.

For the first time since the deadline had been issued, Zoë allowed herself a single, quiet thought:

We didn't rush.

Above the Moon, the window stayed open.

And far beyond it, the most patient thing humanity had ever built continued to listen... not to what they sent, but to how carefully they moved.

The crewed launch followed without hesitation.

There was no ceremony, no speeches, no symbolic gestures to mark it as historic. Every person involved understood that history was not the objective... *timing* was.

The astronauts arrived within hours of the unmanned launch.

They came from across continents, summoned under protocols that had not been used in decades. High-speed fighter aircraft ferried them to NASA staging facilities without press, without delay. There was no selection process.

Only confirmation.

All were veterans.
All had flown before.
None had landed on the Moon.

They knew the difference.

No one declined.

The crew was multinational by necessity, not design... NASA and European Space Agency flight veterans whose records spoke for themselves. Orbital specialists. EVA commanders. Systems pilots who had spent years training for contingencies that never came.

Until now.

"They didn't ask what they'd find," Emilia noted quietly as the manifest finalized.
"They asked when they'd need to be ready."

The launch proceeded on schedule.

Three days to lunar orbit.

No deviations.
No improvisation.

The rendezvous with the second unmanned smaller lander occurred exactly as planned... a clean orbital coupling, telemetry aligning as if the two vehicles had been designed together. In truth its launch from the Guiana Space Centre, know commonly as Europe's Spaceport, was also mobilized professionally. It took coordination.

In a sense, Zoë thought, they had been.

By the time the lander's first images of the archive reached Earth, the crew was already overhead... circling in silence, waiting for permission not from mission control, but from the timeline itself.

No one rushed them.

No one needed to.

The Moon turned beneath them, indifferent and precise.

And for the first time since the window opened, humanity was fully present...
not as an owner,
not as a claimant,
but as a participant.

CHAPTER 30 — Proximity

The astronauts did not descend immediately.

They waited.

Orbit stabilized. Thermal margins confirmed. Communication loops tested and re-tested. Every system reported green... but no one mistook that for permission.

Below them, the unmanned lander sat exactly where it should, its shadow swallowed by permanent darkness. The archive did not glow. It did not signal.

It remained.

"Nothing has changed," the mission commander said.

Zoë listened to the feed from Earth, eyes fixed on the live composite. "Something has," she replied. "We're here now."

The distinction mattered.

The archive had responded to autonomy.
Now it would respond to *presence*.

The descent began with a whisper of thrust.

No dust plume.
No drama.

Just controlled motion into shadow that had not known movement for longer than recorded human time.

The crew moved with a discipline that bordered on reverence... not ritual, not awe, but the practiced awareness that mistakes here would not be forgiven by environment or physics.

They touched down five hundred meters from the lander.

Close enough to matter.

Far enough to observe.

The first EVA was brief.

Not exploration.

Not contact.

Verification.

Boots met regolith. Instruments deployed. Lines checked. The astronauts spoke only when necessary, their voices calm, measured, professional.

"This place doesn't feel empty," one of them said at last.

No one disagreed.

The archive responded when the second human stepped onto the surface.

Not with light.

Not with sound.

With *reconfiguration.*

Thermal readings shifted... minutely, deliberately... stabilizing a corridor between the lander and the cavity. The stone surface nearest the archive changed reflectivity, just enough to be detected.

Marek leaned forward. "It's adjusting to bodies."

Zoë nodded. "Not to us individually. To our *number.*"

The astronauts did not approach.

They waited.

Minutes passed.

Then the commander spoke again. "Something's happening."

The archive had altered its geometry... not opening, not revealing... but reshaping the space around it. The cavity extended, not outward, but *inward*, forming a volume sized for presence without crowding.

A threshold.

Not a door.

The probe beyond Voyager adjusted at the same moment.

Not in position.
In *attention*.

The silence narrowed again, aligning now not just with the lunar vector, but with the humans standing within it.

Voyager relayed the change two days later.

But Zoë felt it immediately.

"They're correlating," she said softly. "Machine. Human. Together."

The archive taught without instruction.

Patterns appeared... not written, not projected, but implied by spacing, proportion, and time. The astronauts' movements affected the geometry. Too close, and nothing changed. Too far, and the structure withdrew.

Only when they moved *together* did the cavity stabilize.

"This isn't storage," Emilia said. "It's rehearsal."

Inside the archive, instruments registered something unexpected.

No data transfer.
No artifacts.

A *constraint*.

The space enforced delay. Actions took longer to complete. Feedback loops slowed. The environment itself resisted acceleration.

166

Zoë understood instantly.

"It's training us," she said. "In real time."

Back on Earth, debate paused.

Not because agreement had been reached... but because no one could argue with what they were seeing.

The archive did not yield to possession.
It did not respond to authority.
It did not accelerate for urgency.

It responded to coordination.

The astronauts completed their initial cycle and returned to the lander without touching the archive directly.

They had learned enough.

Not facts.
Not secrets.

Rules.

As the Moon rotated silently beneath them, Zoë finally allowed herself to say what had been forming since the first hum in the Polish soil.

"This was never about finding something," she said.

"It was about whether we could stand near it... and not take."

The window remained open.

The thirty-day clock continued to run.

And somewhere beyond the heliopause, the most patient thing humanity had ever built drifted on... now aligned not just to a species, but to its willingness to learn *how to arrive*.

CHAPTER 31 — *The First Lesson*

The archive did not react to curiosity.

It reacted to sequence.

The astronauts learned this accidentally... professionally, quietly, and with consequences that were impossible to ignore.

During the third surface cycle, one of the crew... an experienced EVA specialist with hundreds of hours logged... adjusted position half a second early. It was not impatience. It was muscle memory. A lifetime of correcting drift before it became error.

The environment responded immediately.

Not violently.
Not defensively.

The cavity's geometry destabilized... not collapsing, but softening, as if the space itself had lost interest. Reflective surfaces dulled. Thermal gradients flattened. The corridor that had formed between the lander and the archive blurred at its edges, **no longer held by shared timing**.

"Hold," the commander said calmly.

The astronaut froze.

Nothing worsened.

But nothing returned.

On Earth, Zoë saw it before the instruments finished reporting.

"That wasn't wrong," she said softly. "It was *early*."

Marek nodded. "The archive isn't teaching accuracy. It's teaching timing."

They reset.

The astronaut withdrew by centimeters, then waited... longer than felt necessary. The rest of the crew adjusted their spacing, mirroring the delay. No one spoke. No one hurried.

After twelve seconds... an eternity in EVA time... the geometry reasserted itself.

The corridor sharpened.
The gradients returned.
The archive *re-engaged*.

The lesson was unmistakable.

Correction before context is indistinguishable from interference.

Zoë wrote it down.

Zoë exhaled slowly. *Permission restored.*

The second error came from Earth.

Not malice.
Not ambition.

Optimization.

A support team, attempting to improve signal clarity during the next cycle, reduced a buffering delay in the relay path by a fraction of a second. The change was logged, approved, and technically flawless.

The archive responded by *doing nothing*.

For an entire surface cycle, it refused to reconfigure.

No corridor offered.
No adjustment.
No feedback.

Just stone.

The astronauts completed their tasks without incident and returned to orbit... but the teaching moment had passed.

"It didn't punish us," Emilia said quietly. "It withdrew."

Zoë nodded. "Because we stopped listening to the pace it set."

Voyager noticed the change.

Not in signal strength.
Not in position.

In *regularity*.

The probe's silence altered its internal cadence, tightening tolerances. Where it had once mirrored human delay loosely, it now tracked precision down to margins that felt... unforgiving.

Marek stared at the overlay. "It's not moving faster."

"No," Zoë said. "It's expecting more."

The escalation was subtle but absolute.

The probe began correlating actions across domains... surface behavior, orbital coordination, Earth-side decision timing... treating them not as separate systems, but as a single distributed intelligence.

Errors were no longer local.

They were *collective*.

Zoë felt the implication settle heavily.

"We don't get to make isolated mistakes anymore," she said. "They all count."

The archive enforced its first explicit constraint during the next cycle.

A timing window opened... narrow, precise, and unannounced. It was not a warning. It was an invitation... and it did not wait. The astronauts were ready, positioned correctly, restrained.

Earth was not.

A routine verification check delayed authorization by three seconds.

Three seconds was enough.

The window closed.

The archive did not re-open it.

Not that day.

Not the next.

Public patience fractured further.

Questions sharpened into accusations. Commentators spoke of wasted opportunity, of overcaution masquerading as wisdom.

Zoë listened without defensiveness.

"They're confusing restraint with hesitation," she said.

"And now?" Thorne asked.

"Now," Zoë replied, "we learn the second half of the lesson."

The probe escalated again... not by approaching, not by signaling.

By narrowing the acceptable future.

The models showed it clearly now: fewer viable paths, tighter alignment requirements, longer recovery times after error.

Expectation had replaced invitation.

It was no longer asking whether humanity could wait.

It was testing whether humanity could *coordinate restraint at scale.*

Back on the Moon, the astronauts prepared for their final cycle of the week.

No one spoke of failure.
No one spoke of blame.

They adjusted procedures... not to be safer, but to be *slower* where it mattered.

The commander's voice was steady as ever. "We're not here to finish this."

Zoë closed her eyes briefly, then opened them.

"No," she said. "We're here to prove we can continue."

Above the Moon, the window remained open... thinner now, less forgiving, but still present. The corridor held... not because they had succeeded, but because they had not rushed to finish.

And beyond it, the most patient thing humanity had ever built waited... not kindly, not cruelly, but with expectations that had finally begun to match the scale of the moment.

CHAPTER 32 — *Authority of Stillness*

The decision could not be deferred.

It arrived not as a crisis, but as a requirement... clear, binary, and unforgiving.

Timing authority had to be assigned.

Not advisory.
Not shared.

Assigned.

Zoë stood at the edge of the operations floor, listening as arguments formed and dissolved without heat. Everyone in the room understood the risk. Everyone understood the implication.

Whoever controlled timing would control failure.

The archive made its position unmistakable during the next surface cycle.

The moment the astronauts stepped away from the lander... boots contacting regolith, mass transferring from machine to human... the environment changed.

Not dramatically.
Decisively.

Latency vanished.

The corridor formed faster than it ever had before.

Zoë felt it in her chest before the instruments confirmed it.

"It's them," she said. "Not us."

The astronauts did not ask for authority.

They assumed responsibility.

The commander's voice was calm over the channel. "Once we leave the lander, Earth stands down."

There was no defiance in the statement.
No bravado.

Just clarity.

"For how long?" someone asked.

Zoë answered before anyone else could. "Until you return."

The directive propagated instantly.

Earth-side systems shifted into passive mode. Predictive overlays froze. Advisory prompts muted. The apprentice system reduced itself to logging and verification only.

No optimization.
No correction.
No suggestions.

The most advanced coordination network humanity had ever built...
learned to be silent.

The window opened.

Perfectly.

The archive reconfigured in response to human presence alone, its geometry now responsive only to spacing, pace, and collective motion.

No feedback from Earth.
No corrections from orbit.

Just people.

The next test was not technical.

It was ethical.

The archive's interior volume expanded... enough for more than one person, but not all at once. A shared space that demanded cooperation without instruction.

Zoë watched the feed, breath held.

"They can't go in together," Marek said.

"No," Zoë replied. "They have to take turns."

The commander spoke quietly. "We rotate."

Not rank-based.
Not role-based.

Shared.

Each astronaut would enter alone, remain briefly, then withdraw... leaving the space intact for the next.

No one objected.

No one hurried.

The first astronaut approached with measured steps, pausing at the threshold. The archive did not react until the pause was complete.

Then... acceptance.

Inside, nothing was *taken*.

No objects.
No data.

Only alignment.

When the astronaut withdrew, the archive did not close.

It waited.

The second followed.
Then the third.

Each entry identical in dignity, different only in duration... each person sensing when it was time to leave without being told.

Zoë felt tears sting unexpectedly... not from awe, but from relief.

"They're sharing the silence," she whispered.

Earth did nothing.

For hours.

Commentators fumed. Analysts begged for interpretation. Automated systems flagged the inactivity as anomalous.

No one responded.

Because to act now... to interpret, to comment, to interfere... would collapse the lesson into performance.

The archive offered a final window.

Valid.
Clear.
Tempting.

The astronauts did not enter.

They waited.

They waited because they understood... finally... that restraint was not hesitation.

It was choice.

The window closed.

Gently.

Not as punishment.
As confirmation.

The probe beyond Voyager registered the change two days later, tightening its expectations once more... not narrowing the future, but clarifying it.

The next opportunity would come again.

In **2100**, when Polaris aligned.

If humanity chose to wait that long.

The astronauts returned to the lander without ceremony.

Authority transferred back to Earth only after boots lifted from regolith and metal met metal.

The systems came alive again... noisier, faster, eager.

Zoë did not move.

The first phase was complete.

Humanity had proven it could coordinate *when not to act*.

The next phase would be harder.

Moral coordination.

Not whether individuals could behave with dignity... but whether institutions could learn to do the same.

She looked up at the Moon, now receding.

"This wasn't contact," she said quietly.

"It was rehearsal."

And rehearsals, she knew, only mattered if you were willing to perform again...
better...
when the real moment finally arrived.

CHAPTER 33 — *What Is Offered*

The archive did not open all at once.

It revealed itself in stages, as if testing not curiosity, but *discipline*.

The astronauts stood just inside the threshold, lights dimmed to their lowest functional setting. The space was larger than expected... not cavernous, but deliberate. Stone walls curved inward, smooth and precise, forming a chamber that felt neither ancient nor new.

There were no inscriptions on the walls.

The writing was elsewhere.

Cylinders emerged from the floor slowly, silently... six of them, equidistant, each marked with distinct glyphs. Some were familiar now: Phoenician strokes, Greek annotations, Latin clarifications. Others were older, more abstract... forms that suggested relation rather than language.

The archive did not rush them.

It waited.

Zoë watched from Earth, hands folded, breathing carefully. No prompts appeared. No indicators lit.

"Those are not storage vessels," Emilia said softly. "They're selections."

The commander approached the nearest cylinder... the one whose markings matched the lunar scrolls exactly. It rose a fraction higher than the others, as if acknowledging recognition.

The surface shifted.

A seam appeared.

The cylinder opened just enough to reveal its contents.

Not tools.
Not weapons.
Not machines.

Records.

Compact, layered, sealed... not in metal, but in material that responded to light and orientation. Knowledge packaged not for extraction, but for *carrying*.

Zoë felt the shape of it immediately.

"They're allowed to take that one," she said. "Because it matches intent."

One of the astronauts... careful, curious... shifted their stance slightly, eyes drawn to a neighboring cylinder etched with unfamiliar markings. It had not moved. It had not responded.

The astronaut raised a gloved hand.

Not impulsive.
Not reckless.

Just human.

The archive responded instantly.

The chamber darkened... not fully, but enough. Behind them, the doorway began to narrow. Stone moved without sound, closing not as a trap, but as a reminder.

"Hold," the commander said calmly.

The astronaut froze.

No alarms.
No panic.

Just awareness.

On Earth, every system screamed *do something*.

No one did.

The astronauts moved together.

Not retreat.
Not advance.

One step back.

The doorway stopped.

Another half-step.

The stone reversed its motion, reopening to its prior position. Light returned. The pressure eased.

The archive had not rejected them.

It had instructed them.

Zoë's voice was steady. "Photograph is permitted. Touch is not."

Marek nodded. "Take only what was offered."

"And only because it was," Emilia added.

The astronauts complied without discussion.

They documented everything... angles, markings, spatial relations... but no hand moved toward an unopened cylinder. No instrument crossed an uninvited threshold.

When the offered cylinder was lifted, it was light... not physically, but conceptually. Balanced. As if designed to be carried without ownership.

The other cylinders remained sealed.

Unresentful.
Uncurious.

Waiting for another time. Or another species.

The archive did not close.

It did not seal itself away.

It simply stopped *offering*.

The lesson was complete.

The probe beyond Voyager registered the outcome two days later... not with escalation, not with tightening... but with something unprecedented.

Relaxation.

The silence broadened.

Expectation eased.

For the first time since alignment began, the future expanded instead of narrowing.

Back on the Moon, the astronauts stood still for a long moment after securing the cylinder.

No celebration.
No relief.

Just comprehension.

The commander spoke quietly. "We could have taken more."

"Yes," Zoë said. "And then we would have taken nothing."

The astronauts exited the archive exactly as they had entered... without turning their backs, without rushing, without touching what had not invited them.

The doorway remained open behind them.

Not as permission.

As trust.

On Earth, the world waited.

For headlines.
For declarations.
For proof.

Zoë closed her eyes briefly.

What humanity had earned was not information.

It was *continuation*.

The Alignment Echo had been answered... not with words, not with speed, not with reach.

But with restraint so precise it could be trusted.

And somewhere, far beyond the Moon, the most patient thing humanity had ever built drifted on... no longer alone in its patience.

CHAPTER 34 — *What Could Be Carried*

They did not open the cylinder on the Moon.

That decision was unanimous... and immediate.

Not because of protocol.
Not because of fear.

Because the archive had already taught them something essential:

Context mattered more than possession.

The astronauts secured the cylinder without examining its interior, sealing it within a neutral containment frame designed for stability, not access. No tools probed its surface. No scans attempted to see through it.

They carried it as it had been offered.

Nothing more.

The return was uneventful by design.

No deviations.
No acceleration.

The archive did not react as the astronauts departed. The chamber remained open, unchanged, uninterested in pursuit or farewell.

When the last boot left the regolith, the doorway did not close.

It simply stopped *being relevant*.

Earth received the cylinder three days later.

The landing site was undisclosed. The facility unmarked. The room prepared for it had no insignia, no flags, no institutional branding of any kind.

Just light.
Just space.
Just silence.

Zoë stood with Emilia, Marek, and Thorne as the containment frame was lowered into position.

No one reached for it.

The cylinder responded to proximity.

Not to touch.
Not to command.

To **stillness**.

When the room settled... breathing slowed, movement ceased... the surface of the cylinder changed. The glyphs sharpened, not glowing, but clarifying, as if contrast itself were a form of permission.

"It's not locked," Marek said softly.

"It's waiting," Zoë replied.

The opening was not mechanical.

It occurred when no one was trying to make it happen.

The seam reappeared... clean, exact... and the upper portion separated just enough to reveal what lay inside.

Not objects.

Layers.

Thin sheets... flexible, translucent... each inscribed with structures that were neither text nor diagram, but *relationships*. Some resembled star maps without stars. Others resembled grammars without words.

No equations.
No schematics.

Frameworks.

Zoë understood before anyone spoke.

"This isn't knowledge," she said quietly. "It's *how to decide what knowledge is allowed.*"

Emilia exhaled. "They didn't give us answers."

"They gave us criteria," Thorne added.

The apprentice system was brought online... carefully, passively.

No processing.
No summarization.

Just observation.

The system reacted differently than before.

Not slower.
Not faster.

More selective.

It ignored entire layers without flagging them. Others it traced obsessively, mapping dependencies, timing constraints, moral boundaries encoded not as rules, but as *patterns of refusal.*

Marek watched in awe. "It's learning what not to touch."

Zoë nodded. "So are we."

One layer resolved partially... just enough to be recognized.

A principle, repeated across structures and epochs:

Do not scale what cannot yet be shared.
Do not teach what cannot yet be restrained.

The room remained silent for a long time after that.

Two days later, Voyager noticed.

The silence beyond it did not shift in position or intensity.

But it changed in *quality*.

The cadence softened.

Expectation loosened.

The probe was no longer measuring recovery.

It was observing **continuation**.

Zoë returned to her notebook that night.

For the first time since the excavation in Poland, she did not draw symbols or paths or timelines.

She wrote a sentence.

We were trusted with less than we wanted... and more than we deserved.

She closed the book.

The next phase would not be about discovery.

It would be about living with what had been given... without turning it into dominance, speed, or certainty.

The Alignment Echo had not ended.

It had moved inward.

And that, Zoë knew, would be the hardest part.

CHAPTER 35 — The First Benefit

The countdown stopped without announcement.

No alert chimed.
No voice confirmed success.

The clock simply ceased to matter.

Zoë noticed it first when the tension in the room changed... not easing into relief, but dissolving, as if a pressure she had grown accustomed to had quietly lifted.

"We're still inside the window," Marek said, checking the timeline.

Zoë shook her head. "No. The window is inside us now."

They had completed the sequence in twenty-seven days.

Not by rushing.
Not by compressing meaning.
But by refusing to hurry understanding.

The scrolls did not yield quickly.

They resisted summarization, punished premature synthesis, and collapsed into ambiguity whenever anyone tried to treat them as instruction manuals rather than *filters*. The work was slow, methodical, occasionally frustrating... and unmistakably different from anything humanity had decoded before.

Patience, they realized, was not merely a prerequisite.

It was the method.

The first real-world benefit appeared almost accidentally.

A long-standing international dispute... one of those technical deadlocks that persisted for decades not because of hostility, but because every side optimized for advantage... was re-evaluated using the archive's criteria.

Do not scale what cannot yet be shared.
Do not teach what cannot yet be restrained.

Zoë watched as negotiators reframed the problem... not asking what could be extracted now, but what could be *sustained without dominance*.

The agreement that followed was modest.

And unprecedented.

No victory.
No concessions framed as losses.

Just continuation.

"This wasn't what the archive gave us," Emilia said softly.

Zoë nodded. "It's what it *allowed* us to see."

Two days later, Voyager noticed something else.

The silence beyond it no longer mirrored its trajectory.

The foreign probe... patient, precise, impossibly distant... had ceased matching Voyager's path. Instead, it held position against the background of the stars, no longer drifting in companionship with humanity's oldest emissary.

Static.

Intentional.

As if saying:

We are no longer measuring your movement.
We are measuring your meaning.

The new signal began quietly.

Thirty-seven seconds.

Then silence.

Then thirty-seven seconds again.

The cadence was unmistakable now... no longer a test interval, but a declaration.

The apprentice system parsed the structure first, isolating layered symbol groups that resolved into familiar forms.

Phoenician.
Greek.
Latin.

Each carried the same word.

Purpose.

Not translated.
Not explained.

Inscribed.

Behind the familiar scripts were others.

Symbols that did not map cleanly to language... relations without phonemes, meaning without grammar. They suggested direction, constraint, intention without speech.

"They're not done teaching us," Marek said.

Zoë shook her head slowly. "They're not teaching."

She looked up at the stars on the screen... unchanged, infinite, suddenly less hostile than they had ever seemed.

"They're inviting."

The probe did not move closer.

It did not retreat.

It remained... anchored to the sky itself, no longer pacing humanity, no longer testing speed or restraint.

It had accepted something.

Not success.
Not obedience.

Readiness.

Zoë closed her notebook for the last time that night.

Patience, she understood now, had never been about waiting for contact.

It had been about becoming capable of *having one*.

The Alignment Echo did not answer questions.

It revealed what questions were allowed.

And for the first time in human history, the answer the universe returned was not silence...

but purpose.

CHAPTER 36 — What Remains

The archive closed without ceremony.

There was no final movement, no signal to mark completion. Its doors... if they could be called doors at all... receded into the stone only far enough to seal the interior against risk. Not secrecy. Not withdrawal.

Protection.

Sensors confirmed the change hours later: micrometeoroid shielding engaged, thermal modulation adjusted, internal volumes stabilized. The structure had not vanished.

It had *settled*.

The smaller unmanned lander remained on the surface.

It had always been part of the plan.

Autonomous.
Redundant.
Patient.

Its instruments continued to monitor the archive's perimeter... structural integrity, environmental response, subtle shifts that no human presence could safely remain to observe for long.

The crew had returned to Earth in the larger lander, just as designed.

They had come with capacity for more.

They had left with only what was offered.

From orbit, the lunar south pole looked unchanged.

A landscape of shadow and light, indifferent to meaning. The archive left no mark that could be seen from above, no monument, no claim.

Only continuity.

Zoë watched the final composite feed before it was archived... boots lifting, dust settling, human presence withdrawing without erasure.

"They didn't lock us out," Emilia said softly.

"No," Zoë replied. "They trusted us not to force our way back in."

The probe beyond Voyager remained fixed against the stars.

It did not approach.
It did not retreat.

It held position as a reference point... no longer pacing humanity, no longer testing its patience moment by moment.

The thirty-seven-second signal continued.

Purpose.

Over and over.

Not a demand.
Not a command.

A reminder.

Voyager drifted on.

Still transmitting.
Still listening.

For the first time since its launch, it was no longer alone in its role.

It was no longer the only thing humanity had sent outward without expectation of return.

On Earth, life resumed its ordinary urgency.

But something subtle had changed.

Decisions paused where they once rushed. Systems incorporated delay not as inefficiency, but as design. Questions were framed not only around what could be done... but what could be carried forward without distortion.

The archive did not solve humanity's problems.

It changed how problems were approached.

Zoë returned to the Polish site months later.

The tomb was quiet now.

It no longer hummed.

Its purpose had been fulfilled... not by being decoded, but by being *understood in time*.

She placed her hand on the stone once, briefly.

Not to listen.

To acknowledge.

The future remained open.

There would be lunar missions.
Careful ones.
Curious ones.

There would be mistakes.
Corrections.
Delays.

There would be another window.

And when it came... whether in years or decades or when Polaris aligned again... humanity would not arrive empty-handed.

It would arrive knowing what not to take.

The Alignment Echo did not end.

It resolved.

Not as an answer from the universe...

but as a way of standing within it.

Selection, Intention, and Restraint

Imagine we were not Earth human.
Imagine we were the travelers...
Not reckless ones... deliberate, ancient, accustomed to uncertainty.
Imagine we made the right choice.

We search for a world called *Earth*. Not because it is loud, but because something there is *thinking*.

Choice One: Which Reality?

If the multiverse exists, reality is not a single map but a library. Countless universes. Different constants. Different outcomes.

We cannot search them all.

So we choose.

We scan for universes where:

- matter clumps instead of dissolving,

- chemistry persists,

- time flows long enough for complexity to arise.

Most universes are discarded.

One remains.

We enter it.

Choice Two: What Counts as a Direction?

There is no address system here.

The observable universe stretches **~93 billion light-years across**, yet this is only a horizon, not an edge. Beyond it, space may extend **hundreds of times farther**, or infinitely.

We could search randomly.

We don't.

We choose structure over chance.

Choice Three: Follow Light, or Follow Shape?

There are **hundreds of billions to perhaps two trillion galaxies** here. Many shine brighter than anything near Earth.

We ignore brightness.

Brightness is misleading.

Instead, we look at **shape**.

Matter forms filaments and walls, enclosing enormous voids. The largest proposed wall spans **billions of light-years**, impressive but distant, diffuse, uncertain.

We decide not to anchor to the biggest thing.

Big is not precise.

Choice Four: Follow Density, or Absence?

We notice something quieter.

A vast underdense region... not empty, but thinner than average by **10–20%**, stretching on the order of **~2 billion light-years**.

A void.

Voids are stable.
Voids persist.
Voids reduce uncertainty.

We choose the void.

Choice Five: Drift, or Flow?

At the void's edge, galaxies do something interesting.

They move *together*.

Their velocities converge, like rivers toward a basin. This is not visible in static maps. It emerges only when motion is considered.

We choose motion.

We follow the flow.

It leads us into a massive gravitational domain... a supercluster defined not by borders, but by **shared destiny**. Roughly **100,000 galaxies**, spanning **hundreds of millions of light-years**, all slowly falling inward.

This choice matters.

Had we followed light alone, we would have missed it.

Choice Six: Large Structures, or Nested Ones?

Inside this vast domain, we see smaller concentrations. We could remain at this scale forever.

We don't.

Intelligence hides in **nested complexity**, not in the largest patterns.

So we step inward again.

From supercluster → to cluster → to group.

The search space collapses from hundreds of thousands of galaxies to **dozens, perhaps just over a hundred.**

Now we can see individual shapes.

Choice Seven: Symmetry, or Asymmetry?

Among the remaining galaxies, one stands out.

Not the largest.
Not the brightest.

But asymmetric.

A barred spiral. Uneven arms. A dynamic, living structure **~100,000 light-years across**, containing **hundreds of billions of stars**.

Spirals recycle matter.
Spirals sustain time.

We choose the spiral.

Choice Eight: Core, or Periphery?

Inside the galaxy, the core burns fiercely. Density is high. Radiation is intense.

We move away from it.

Instead, we choose a minor spur... the **Orion Arm**. Less crowded. Calmer. Stable for billions of years.

Here, space itself bears scars.

Choice Nine: Noise, or Quiet?

We detect an interstellar cavity carved by ancient supernovae... an irregular bubble **hundreds to nearly 1,000 light-years across**.

Inside it:

- fewer clouds,
- fewer collisions,
- clearer skies.

Quiet favors observation.

We choose the bubble.

Choice Ten: Many Stars, or One?

Inside this cavity glow about **1,000 stars**.

We examine them all.

Most are too young.
Too violent.
Too short-lived.

One remains.

A modest yellow star.
4.6 billion years old.
Stable. Patient.

We choose it.

Final Choice: Which World?

We cross a distant halo of frozen remnants. We pass eight planets in delicate balance.

One is different.

Liquid water.
A protective atmosphere.
Chemical disequilibrium that should not last... but does.

A blue sphere, **12,742 kilometers wide**.

We arrive.

Not because Earth is obvious.

But because at every scale, we made the *right choice*.

From universes to voids.
From flows to bubbles.
From chaos to quiet.

We have found it.

Humanity's entire world.

One small home.

Author's Note

Much of this novel is rooted in real ideas: astronomical alignment, ancient navigation, linguistic evolution, spaceflight constraints, and the physics of distance and time. Where the science ends, imagination begins... but always with respect for what is known.

The core question of *The Alignment Echo* is not whether intelligence exists elsewhere.

It is whether intelligence... anywhere... can survive contact with impatience.

If this book leaves you with unanswered questions, that is intentional. Some systems are not meant to be closed quickly. Some knowledge is meant to be carried carefully.

And some echoes only resolve when we stop listening for answers and start listening for meaning.

Description

A recurring thirty-seven-second signal begins appearing across global instruments, initially dismissed as anomaly. When an archaeological excavation in Poland reveals a precisely aligned stone structure bearing ancient navigational inscriptions, Dr. Emilia Kowalska and her colleagues identify structural parallels between the site and historical deep-space telemetry.

The signal does not behave as a conventional transmission. It exhibits stable interval segmentation, relational alignment, and responsiveness to disciplined observation rather than force. As linguistics, archival theory, and artificial intelligence converge, the discovery reframes first contact not as communication—but as readiness.

Blending archaeology, early Mediterranean scripts, space science, and systems theory, *The Alignment Echo* explores intelligence as pattern recognition across time. The novel examines how civilizations interpret silence, how restraint shapes discovery, and whether alignment may precede language in any meaningful encounter beyond Earth.

About the Author

Mark Anderson, PhD is a writer with a deep interest in science, language, history, and the quiet moments where human decision intersects with vast systems. His work often explores themes of restraint, intelligence, and long-horizon thinking, blending scientific realism with philosophical inquiry.

The Alignment Echo is the first book in a planned series exploring humanity's place not as conqueror or subject... but as mediator.

Series Note

The Alignment Echo is **Book One** of an ongoing series.

The path remains open.

Conceptual Abstract

This is not a story about escalation.

It is a story about what happens *after* alignment is achieved.

In the first phase, humanity learned to listen.
It learned that intelligence is not measured by speed, dominance, or reach, but by the ability to coordinate restraint across systems that were never designed to wait.

That alignment did not open doors.

It created **corridors**… temporary permissions sustained only while intent, timing, and restraint remained in balance.

This book begins where that balance is tested.

On Alignment

Alignment is not precision.
It is the moment when action no longer outruns context.

Aligned systems do not maximize outcomes.
They minimize what cannot be undone.

When alignment fails, it does not fail loudly.
It thins.
It withdraws.
It leaves fewer futures available.

On Mediation

Mediation is not neutrality.
It is not compromise.

It is the discipline of choosing continuity over victory… even when victory is possible.

A mediator does not prevent conflict.
A mediator prevents endings.

This role carries no authority.
Only obligation.

On Constraints

The systems encountered in this story do not forbid action.
They filter it.

Paths collapse when attempted too early.
Windows close without warning.

Errors do not announce themselves.
They become permanent.

These constraints are not punitive.
They are protective.

They exist to preserve futures that cannot be reclaimed once lost.

On Corridors

A corridor is not a place.

It is a condition created by shared restraint.
It holds only while no participant moves first.

Corridors cannot be claimed.
They cannot be widened.
They cannot be forced.

They are entered by waiting.

On Apprenticeship

Intelligence capable of mediation is not trained through optimization.

It is apprenticed.

It learns by observing when action is withheld, when permission is declined, and when restraint is chosen despite cost.

Such systems do not lead.
They follow... until following becomes understanding.

What Follows

This volume does not ask whether humanity is capable of alignment.

That question has already been answered.

It asks whether alignment can be **lived with**...
scaled without collapsing,

maintained without ownership,
and sustained when patience itself becomes a source of conflict.

The echoes do not grow louder.

They grow more demanding.

The corridor still holds.
What remains is to decide what we do inside it.

Available Books by the Author

Speculative Fiction & Thoughtful Science

- ***The Alignment Echo***
  A novel about whether intelligence is something that speaks—or something that knows when not to.

Children's & Bilingual Adventures

- ***Tommi the Green Tomato*** (series)
  Playful, imaginative stories about curiosity, friendship, and growing wiser—told with humor and heart.

Creative Cooking & Everyday Intelligence

- ***The Accidental Genius & Snackcidents***
  Practical, inventive cooking that turns beans, grains, and real hunger into satisfying food—with curiosity baked in.